PERIL IN THE BLOOMS

PERIL IN THE BLOOMS

PARKS PAT MYSTERIES
BOOK FIFTEEN

P.D. WORKMAN

 PD WORKMAN

ISBN: 9781774688557 (KDP Paperback)
ISBN: 9781774688564 (KDP Hardcover)
ISBN: 9781774688588 (Lulu Paperback)
ISBN: 9781774688571 (Large Print)
ISBN: 9781774688595 (Digital)
ISBN: 9781774688601 (Auto-narrated audiobook)

ALSO BY P.D. WORKMAN

MYSTERY/SUSPENSE:

Parks Pat Mysteries
Police Procedural Set in Canada
Out with the Sunset
Long Climb to the Top
Dark Water Under the Bridge
Immersed in the View
Skimming Over the Lake
Hazard of the Hills
Knows the Hills
Spanning the Creek
Sanctuary in the Stream
Echoes of the Engine
Bench with a View
Beneath the Icy Depths
Grounded in the Wind
Reservoir of Secrets
Peril in the Blooms

Kenzie Kirsch Medical Thrillers
Unlawful Harvest
Doctored Death
Dosed to Death

Gentle Angel

Rushin' Death

Posed for Death

Death of a Corpse

Endowed with Death

Shattered to Death

Captured in Death

Currying Death

Healed to Death

Death's Charm

Bleeding Hearts Valley Thrillers
An Abrupt Departure

High-Tech Crime Solvers Series
Virtually Harmless

Cowritten with D. D. VanDyke
California Corwin P. I. Mystery Series
The Girl in the Morgue

Stand Alone Suspense Novels
Looking Over Your Shoulder

Lion Within

Pursued by the Past

In the Tick of Time

Loose the Dogs

AND MORE AT PDWORKMAN.COM

To the keepers of knowledge and wisdom

STYLE NOTE

Since my largest readership is in the USA, I have chosen to use US spellings throughout this series. That includes the Americanization of centre to center, even where it is an actual place name, just for consistency's sake. I apologize to my Canadian readers for this.

I have chosen, however, to use Canadian grammar, particularly for Canadian voices. If you see what you think is a grammar error, it may just be Canadian, eh?

CHAPTER ONE

*I*t was a beautiful day. The morning was pleasant, the heat of the day not yet kicking in. Margie was sure that by midafternoon, it would be too hot to spend much time outside, but the ceremonies would be over by then, and she would be back at home or at the air-conditioned office if she decided to go in for the afternoon.

Moushoom, sitting in his wheelchair with a blanket across his lap, would be back to his temperature-controlled bedroom. She was glad that they had decided to go to the reopening of the botanical gardens together. Moushoom always seemed ten times better after spending time outside in the fresh air. Like Antaeus, the Titan in Greek mythology who gained strength from contact with the earth. That was Moushoom, gathering strength when he was in contact with nature. He remembered all the old stories, all that he had learned at the sides of his parents and grandparents back before modern technology.

When she had heard about the opening of the newly refreshed gardens at Riley Park, she hadn't thought much of

1

it initially. What she remembered of Riley Park from when she was a child visiting Calgary was the wading pool.

Until then, a "wading pool" had meant that little round, blow-up kiddie pool that her family had filled with the garden hose. Too cold to put her feet into when it was first filled up, and then warming in the sun. The pristine water getting clouded with leaves and grass clippings and bugs as she and her cousins hopped in and out of it throughout the day.

The wading pool at Riley Park was something different altogether. It was a vast concrete structure, constantly filtered and refilled like a swimming pool, with all those curves and dips and hills, filled with laughing, shrieking children and lounging adults trying to escape the heat. It had seemed enormous to her at the time, and she wondered whether her memory was accurate.

Back then, she hadn't even been aware of any gardens. There had been a small playground with a swing set, slide, and rusting animal shapes mounted on springs. There were huge trees and a lone squirrel that ran along the telephone wires back before the gray squirrel population in Calgary had exploded and squirrels were everywhere. She didn't remember any gardens.

Now there was a large, colorful playground full of climbing equipment, slides, and a saucer swing. And there was an adult playground with parallel bars, a climbing net, and various other equipment that Margie would have to read the instructions to know how to use.

"We used to come here to watch cricket," Moushoom told her as she pushed his wheelchair along the pathway. Margie had been staring at the different varieties of trees, trying to identify each one. She had no idea what most of them were. She identified an oak tree by the wavy shape of its leaves. And a maple. But most of them, she was clueless about. One of them was full of red fruit that looked like cherries. Did cherries grow in Alberta? Big ones like that, not the little chokecherries she was familiar with?

Stella strained on the leash, wanting to go everywhere, to smell everything. There was a whole world of sights and scents that needed to be cataloged.

"Cricket?" Margie repeated, wondering if Moushoom was feeling all right. Who would watch cricket in Calgary? She wondered whether he meant a different sport, or if he had been watching cricket on TV at the home and was confusing it with reality.

"Yes. Big cricket pitch over there," Moushoom waved with one hand.

"Oh, is there?"

There was a large green field. Margie supposed it could have been used for cricket or soccer. But there were no stands. No soccer goalposts. She couldn't see any field of play marked out in the grass.

They made their way around the trees on the paved pathway, and the wading pool came into view. It was huge, with curves sprawling across the park. There was a splash park that hadn't been there when she was a child. At least, not that she could remember. She was glad the wading pool really was big, and that it hadn't just been a childhood memory with everything out of scale.

"Wow, look at it. I can't believe how big it is."

"We brought so many grandchildren and cousins to this pool," Moushoom remembered. "They always had a great time."

"Unless there were wasps," Margie recalled. "I remember one year there was a huge number of wasps. They were everywhere."

"Did you get stung?"

"No."

It was funny that the wading pool had not triggered Margie's fear of the water. But then, it wasn't more than two feet deep anywhere. She didn't have to worry about drowning in it, about not being able to touch the bottom, the water closing over her head. It had been a fun, safe place to play, no more dangerous than the bathtub.

The pathway wound around the pool to the other side, where Margie saw a clubhouse of some kind.

"Cricket," Moushoom repeated.

Margie pushed the wheelchair around the building.

CALGARY & DISTRICT
  CRICKET LEAGUE
  (1908)

Margie laughed. "Cricket," she agreed. "Did you like the games? Were they fun to watch?"

He nodded. "Some of those bowlers... you wouldn't believe how fast they can throw."

Margie could see someone practicing, throwing ball after ball. She wouldn't have wanted to be in the path of that cannon.

"It looks like the opening is happening over here," she motioned to a flat area where folding chairs had been set up. There was a podium at the front and a few men were setting up speakers.

"Push me right up to the front," Moushoom instructed. "I want to be able to see everything."

"Okay," Margie laughed and agreed. There would be no sitting in the back and staying anonymous today.

CHAPTER TWO

*T*ents and shades had been set up around the gardens to keep them out of sight until the big reveal. But other smaller gardens were already visible. They were filled with a riot of color, orange and red and purple and yellow. Margie stopped beside one to take in the individual flowers and watch the bees buzzing around them.

"These are amazing," she said. "Look at all of the different kinds of flowers."

"Some of these were in my kokum's garden," Moushoom told her, speaking of his own grandmother. Margie's great-great-grandmother. Margie had only seen pictures of her; they had never met. Moushoom's mother had been alive when Margie was born, but had died soon after. Margie had no recollection of her either. She only came alive in Moushoom's stories.

"She knew her medicine," Moushoom told Margie. "She always had just the herbs the family needed close at hand. And enough for friends and neighbors, too. She took care of people."

"How did she know how to use them? From her mother?"

"Many generations of mothers," Moushoom agreed. "All of the stories and herblore passed down through the generations. There was no pharmacy to run to then, only to Mother Earth. She taught us what we needed to know."

Margie maneuvered Moushoom's wheelchair across the grass. It was a lot more difficult than using the paved pathway, but she didn't have far to go.

"Can I put my grandfather here?" she asked a pinch-faced middle-aged woman who was giving the sound men directions.

The woman looked at her, frowning, and then around the chairs that had been set up. "Didn't anyone leave space for wheelchairs?" she demanded.

The other busy employees in matching blue t-shirts looked around at each other, shaking heads.

"Oh, good grief." The woman marched over and pulled a chair out of line at either end of the front two rows to make space for wheelchair seating. "Please. If that isn't enough space, take another one out," she told Margie.

Margie nodded her thanks and pushed Moushoom's wheelchair into place. She tied Stella's leash to the arm of the wheelchair. The woman gave more instructions to the various employees working on getting everything set up. They seemed to be running a little late, as people were already gathering and talking.

The woman finished and approached Margie. She looked at Moushoom in the wheelchair.

"Is this one of our special guests?" she asked. "I am Dr. Eliza Thorndyke." She offered a dry, thin hand for each of them to shake.

"No, we just came for the opening," Margie told her. "It looked interesting and it's been forever since I have been to

Riley Park, so we thought we would come along and have a look."

"Well, welcome, I'm glad you could make it." Her eyes kept returning to Moushoom. "We have a land acknowledgment at the beginning of the ceremony. I would like to make sure that your people are mentioned. What tribe…?"

"We are Métis," Margie said, her cheeks warming. This was not territory she had navigated often.

"We acknowledge Treaty 7. Are you included in Treaty 7?"

"No," Moushoom said strongly. "We did not sign the Treaty."

Thorndyke nodded. "Right, of course. I should know that, I'm sure. Should I just include… the Métis people, or is there a specific organization…?"

"We are Métis," Moushoom said. "We don't need a number."

Margie was aware that Calgary fell into District 5 and 6, but she didn't know which Riley Park was in. Besides, the districts were not the way the Métis identified. They were simply for governance.

"I'll be sure to include you in the land acknowledgment," Thorndyke said. She scurried to the podium and flipped through pages, a pen held in one hand as she scowled down at what was written and scratched in some changes. Margie looked at Moushoom, and he shrugged. It was weird how these land acknowledgments had become a thing at every public event. Margie wasn't sure how she felt about them or if they had any real meaning.

After a few minutes, as the speakers for the opening sat down in a row behind the podium, Thorndyke leaned in to the microphone and tapped it, creating a noise on the speakers that made everyone jump, and several cover their ears.

"Could everyone take their seats?" Thorndyke suggested, satisfied that the sound system was working. "We will get started shortly."

The audience chairs started to fill. It was easy to see that they had not anticipated such a large gathering. There were few empty chairs, and a number of people stood in the back or around the sides to watch.

Thorndyke looked at her watch and began, speaking too close to the microphone and again blasting everyone's eardrums.

"I am gratified to see so many people here today who are interested in preserving and expanding the gardens. These plants and flowers do more than just provide the eye with beauty. They are vital to the health of the environment and to us individually."

She paused to give them all a big smile. It looked forced. It looked like it was something she had been coached to do rather than being normal and natural. Margie suspected it was written into her script: STOP AND SMILE.

"We acknowledge that we are on Treaty 7 territory and the traditional land of the Métis people. We acknowledge and respect the histories, languages, and diverse cultures of the First Nations who traditionally live, work, and play on this land."

Another pause and smile.

There was a sharp report that made Margie first tense in her seat, looking around, and then jump to her feet. She looked at Dr. Thorndyke, who was looking startled and confused. Margie could just see the pant leg of her tan pants around the podium, suddenly stained red at the thigh.

Margie turned around, scanning the throng behind her, who at first were frozen in place, and then dissolved into chaos. A figure wearing a ball cap and hoodie broke into a run, heading away from the crowd and toward the edge of the park. Margie sprinted after him.

It was a few long seconds before the crowd started to clue in to what had just happened and started making noise. There were some screams and cries of distress, but no more gunshots. Margie had made a split-second decision to pursue the fleeing man rather than staying behind to look for any more attackers or provide first aid to Dr. Thorndyke. There were a lot of people present. Someone else would have first aid knowledge. They would all have cell phones and could call 9-1-1. The fact the man was running away meant that he was probably alone and no further violence was intended. The biggest risk was losing him because she had not acted quickly enough.

Margie had started running in the mornings before work, when she could get herself up early enough. But jogging, not sprinting. Good for cardio, good to get the blood flowing and get some benefit from it—but she had never been fast, even in foot races as a child. Certainly not now, putting in too much time behind a desk and eating too much fast food and pasta.

She kept the man in view as long as she could, cataloging every detail she could. Height. Build. Coloring. What he was wearing from head to foot. He wasn't carrying anything. She couldn't tell whether he still had the gun or not, and Margie didn't have hers. She was off duty, on an outing with her grandfather to look at the gardens; of course she wasn't armed. It was Canada.

The whole thing was over in a couple of minutes. The man made it out of the park and across the street, and Margie was trailing behind him, too slow, losing him in the traffic and between the parked cars. He might have made it into one of the buildings; she hadn't seen. But she had lost him.

She stopped running and pulled out her phone, dialing 9-1-1. She hoped everybody at the park hadn't called at once and overwhelmed the dispatchers.

"This is Detective Patenaude," she identified herself quickly once she reached the emergency operator. "I was at Riley Park at the shooting. Pursued the shooter but lost him. I am at…" Margie looked at the street signs and read them off to the dispatcher. "He is on foot in this area, within a block or two. If you can get a perimeter up fast enough, you might still be able to catch him. Suspect is wearing a black hoodie, Flames ball cap, blue jeans, white sneakers. The hood was pulled up over his head, but he might have removed it to change his appearance after getting out of my sight."

She stopped for a moment to catch her breath and let the dispatcher get all of that down and start dispatching units. "I did not get a good look at the suspect's face, but he appeared to be a slimly built male, light-skinned, around six feet tall. May still be armed. He's been running, so he may be out of breath. He was fast." She blew out her breath again, wishing she had been able to catch him or get a better description.

"Stay where you are, detective," the dispatcher told her. "A unit will come to talk to you, so you can give him more information about the suspect's speed and direction."

Margie had turned around to return to the park, but she stopped and stayed where she was. It would only be a minute or two before the car got to her, and maybe they could catch the shooter before he got away.

She took deep breaths. Her chest was burning. It had been a much harder run than what she was used to.

CHAPTER THREE

a couple of patrol officers stopped to talk to Margie, and she pointed out the direction she had last seen the suspect heading and a couple of possibilities as to where he might have gone when she had lost track of him. Margie recounted the pursuit and description again, repeating details until they were sure they had all of the information she could give them. Then she headed back to the park.

Everything seemed much farther than it had a few minutes earlier. Margie had covered more distance than she had thought. That was something, at least.

Not much time had passed. She had felt like she had been talking to the patrol officers forever, but as she arrived at the park, emergency vehicles were just starting to pull in.

She didn't have to worry about talking her way past a cop stationed to keep everyone away from the crime scene, because no perimeter or check point had been set up yet. She was one of the first law enforcement officers to get there. And she knew exactly where she was going without talking to anyone. She marched quickly to the seat she had abandoned.

For a moment, her heart froze as she stared at the empty

wheelchair. Had something happened to Moushoom? Had he been hurt too? If she had improperly assessed the risk and he had gotten hurt because of it...

But even as she was thinking dire, panicky thoughts, she was also looking around to figure out what had happened since she had run away, leaving Moushoom, an injured victim, and everyone else behind.

Looking up at the raised platform the podium was on, Margie could see Dr. Thorndyke sitting up and talking. That was a good sign. Then she identified the back of the man kneeling beside her.

Moushoom.

Margie hurried forward. The other speakers and sound technicians attempted to keep her from coming onto the stage, but Margie shook her head and used her commanding cop voice.

"Step aside, please, make a space. I'm a law enforcement officer and first responder."

They quickly moved aside and let her step up onto the platform. What Margie saw when she looked down at Thorndyke almost made her laugh aloud.

Moushoom's proudly worn Métis sash was no longer tied around his waist, but around the wound in Dr. Thorndyke's thigh.

"How is the patient?" she asked Moushoom, kneeling beside him.

Moushoom turned his head to look at her and smiled. "So you decided to come back, daughter."

"Yes. Didn't manage to catch the shooter."

"You should have stayed to help the wounded."

"It looks like you had that under control. I had to try."

"One bullet," Moushoom told her what she already knew. "In the fleshy part of the thigh. Missed the bone and artery. Bullet is still in there."

Margie nodded. She didn't reach over to touch the dressed wound. Best to leave it alone until the EMTs got there. The ambulance was already pulling into the park, the police having given the "all clear" after confirming there were no more shooters and it was safe.

One paramedic approached with a medical case.

"This the only injury?"

"Yes. One shot, one hit. My first aider here says no bone or artery involvement."

Moushoom nodded solemnly. The paramedic looked down at the sash.

"Is this yours? Is it… a scarf?"

He was undoubtedly wondering why anyone would be wearing a scarf in the middle of the summer, even if it was in the cool of the morning.

"A sash," Moushoom told him. "The Métis sash is a tool with many uses, one of which is to bandage wounds."

"Uh, okay. Lucky you had one with you, then. We'll just take a look here, and I'll use some sterile dressings to redress it for transport."

"You should leave it tied until she gets to the hospital," Moushoom told him disapprovingly. "The more times you disturb the wound, the more she is going to bleed."

The paramedic frowned at this. He poked around the edges of the sash. "It looks like there was a good amount of bleeding."

"And the sash has stopped it. So you can transport her safely. The surgeon can take off the sash when he is ready to stitch her up."

The paramedic motioned to his partner to come up to the platform. "I appreciate what you have done. You should go sit back down until the police are ready to question you."

Moushoom looked at Margie, and she nodded. "You did good, Moushoom."

He patted her hand and attempted to get to his feet. He failed to get up on his own. Margie knew she was strong enough to help him up, but then she would also have to help him down from the platform and walk him to his wheelchair. While he had gotten from his wheelchair to the injured Dr. Thorndyke on his own, his legs were tired now and he didn't have the adrenaline of an emergency to give him a boost.

She knew he would prefer not to appear feeble in front of all these people, even if he needed the wheelchair to get back out of the park.

"Moushoom," she said respectfully, "instead of getting up this way, why don't you swing your legs off the platform, and I will bring your chair over." She pointed. "Then you can just slide right into it."

Moushoom's eyes lit up. A fan of wrinkles pointed up from his eyes and mouth. "I can do that," he assured her.

She touched his shoulder and left him there to maneuver independently while she fetched the wheelchair. By the time she got it positioned beside the stage, Moushoom had managed to move into a seated position, dangling his legs off the side, and she just softened his descent as he slid from the stage into the chair. Moushoom grinned up at her.

"Easy as pie."

"Where's Stella?" It wasn't until then that Margie noticed the dog was no longer tied to the wheelchair.

"She wasn't about to let me go far on my own," Moushoom told her. He gave a little whistle, and Stella came running from behind the stage to his side. He patted her head and scratched her ears. "She thinks I need to be watched."

Margie spread the blanket over Moushoom's legs again. "Are you comfy?"

"I'm fine," he told her.

Margie turned her head to look at Dr. Thorndyke, who

was complaining to the paramedics about something, her hands over her stomach. One of them pulled back just as she turned to the side and threw up, barely missing him.

"It's just the shock," the paramedic assured her. "You'll feel better soon. Just try to relax. We'll get you into the ambulance and—"

Dr. Thorndyke's mouth opened, but no words came out. Margie leaned closer as if that might clarify everything. She thought she would hear Dr. Thorndyke gasping, but she couldn't hear any breathing, labored or otherwise. The medics moved in quickly, repositioning her, asking her urgent questions, listening with their stethoscopes and throwing ideas and instructions back and forth as they tried to deal with the new symptoms. One of them brought the gurney from the ambulance, and they hurriedly transferred her to it and then into the ambulance, away from the sight of gawking onlookers. One of them stayed with her while the other went to the front of the ambulance to drive.

"Is she breathing?" Margie asked as he passed her.

"Sorry, ma'am, can't comment."

"I'm a police detective. The first one on the scene, so this is my site until I release it. Is she breathing?"

He gave his head a quick shake. "We'll try to get her back," he said grimly, opening his door. "But it happened so fast."

"Do you think it was shock from the gunshot wound?"

The paramedic turned his key in the ignition. "We're doing what we can for her, detective. Someone will let you know."

"If it is a homicide rather than an assault, I'll need to know right away."

He gave another nod and pulled out, the lights and siren turning on as he drove away from her.

CHAPTER FOUR

*A*fter the ambulance left, there was not much for Margie to do. She cleared everybody from the platform and asked them to remain in the front row of the audience seating so they were handy for police interviews. She kept everyone else off the stage and took pictures, getting a few different perspectives. She took pictures of where she thought the shooter had been standing as well, and then went and stood close to the spot to take a few photos of the empty podium. She looked down at the ground, but the thick grass obscured any footprints and concealed anything that might have fallen from the shooter's pockets.

Margie spoke with the various law enforcement officers who had answered the dispatcher's call for assistance, arranging for the podium and shooter's position to be cordoned off. She was sure that some witnesses had left, but most of the crowd was still hanging around to see what would happen and if the opening of the gardens would eventually continue.

A man in a pressed white shirt and tie approached Margie. "Am I to understand that you are in charge?"

"Until I am told otherwise," Margie agreed. "At the moment, I'm just trying to preserve the scene until the appropriate people arrive."

"My name is Henry Milton, from Calgary Parks. I'm sorry if this sounds insensitive after what has happened here, but are we going to be able to have our opening today? If we stay out of the area you have taped off and move the sound equipment somewhere else..." He motioned toward the tents covering the gardens to be revealed. "Can we continue with an abbreviated ceremony, let people in to see the gardens...? Or is that going to cause all kinds of complications for your investigation?"

"I'm afraid it is not going to go ahead today. And I've asked those who may have seen what happened to sit over here..." Margie indicated the front row the other VIPs were sitting on. "If you are in charge of the event, we might have some questions for you, so I'd like it if you would stick around here for a bit."

"Oh, I wasn't in charge of it." He shook his head, face turning a little pink, "I'm just the pretty face reading a script on behalf of the city. I had very little to do with the planning."

"Who was in charge of the opening?"

"Well..." He looked at the empty podium. "Eliza Thorndyke was the major force behind it. I'm sure she had plenty of help from others in the various organizations we were dealing with, but if you want the person who knew everything that was going on and was in charge of keeping all of the parts moving smoothly... that was Dr. Thorndyke."

"I was afraid you were going to say that."

"Yes," Milton bowed his head for a moment. "It is shocking. I don't understand how something like this could happen. Why it would happen. I mean... they are flower beds. Who shoots someone at the opening of botanical gardens?"

"It's pretty bizarre," Margie had to agree. "Maybe it was just a random thing. Or intended to cause disruption. There were a lot of people here. He might have intended to hit a different target."

"But over *flowers?*"

"I don't know. There may have been a different reason for it. The doctor's personal life. Family situation…?" she trailed off, inviting Milton to offer his thoughts.

"I don't know. I don't know anything about Dr. Thorndyke's life outside the Hillhurst Botanical Research Institute."

Margie reached for her notepad, but wasn't dressed for work and hadn't put it into her pocket. She pulled out her phone instead.

"I just need to start making notes of the names and organizations," she told Milton. "Sorry. I don't want to forget anything. So, she was in charge of this institute?"

"Well, it's not as big and grand as it sounds. I think Eliza was the only employee. Everyone else was contract, on an as-needed basis. But she was able to get grants for research projects… which are related to the gardens we were opening today. They are each focused on research being done by the Institute."

"Really? Like what?"

"Well… the usefulness of various flowers and herbs. Not just for decorative or culinary uses but medicinal. Research on pollination and ways to keep crop returns healthy with the reduction in pollinators in the environment. There are many ways that they can do research on a small scale that will have much larger implications."

Margie nodded. "Got it. I have someone I have to talk

to, so if you could please have a seat with the others, I will get back to you shortly."

Margie watched to make sure he would do as she asked and then transferred her gaze to Detective Cruz, who joined her.

"You've had quite the morning, Detective Pat," he observed.

"I have,"

"*Parks* Pat," he nudged.

"Maybe I should do like Dr. Galt said and stay away from parks, since it seems like I am attracting the bodies—the cases—lately."

Margie didn't know what to think of the nickname anymore. After investigating a few homicides in park settings, she had been saddled with the nickname and the reputation of possessing some kind of expertise in solving such cases. And since she kept getting called out to murders in parks, the idea was just reinforced.

But the unfortunate experience of actually being in a park when something violent occurred had happened to her a number of times. Was she somehow *manifesting* the murders? Causing them to happen?

She knew it wasn't possible, but it had happened enough times that she was getting a bit paranoid about it. Maybe she should do a smudging or ask Moushoom for his help in ridding her of the evil spirits that seemed to plague her.

"So, walk me through what happened," Cruz suggested.

Like Margie, the pleasant Filipino cop mostly investigated homicides. She swallowed. "Does that mean it is now a homicide?" she asked. "I don't have a radio," so I haven't heard what has been announced.

Cruz nodded. "Dr. Eliza Thorndyke was dead on arrival at the hospital. They said that she was here," he indicated the platform, "when she drew her last breath."

"It's true," Margie agreed. "Dr. Thorndyke seemed to be doing really well, just a little stunned by what had happened. And then she started complaining about other symptoms, not feeling well—I didn't hear all of what was said—you'll have to ask the paramedics—and she vomited. And she stopped breathing. I wasn't close enough to be sure. By the time they had her in the ambulance... the paramedic who was driving confirmed that she was no longer breathing."

Cruz's brows were furrowed. He shook his head. "She died from a leg wound? And it didn't hit the artery or anything?"

"I don't think so. Moushoom patched her up while I was chasing the shooter. He said the bullet hadn't hit bone or artery, and he had it tied up tightly. Wouldn't let the paramedics unwrap it in case it started bleeding again. I was there. I didn't see blood soaking through or seeping out somewhere else. If she had died from blood loss... there would have been a lot more blood. You can go look at the platform by the podium there where she was shot. There is hardly any. If she bled out, there would be pools of it."

Cruz glanced toward the stage and nodded. He would do a full scene survey and see for himself, but he trusted that what Margie was telling him was accurate.

"It must have been something else... the shock... something in her body that just shut down. Maybe she had a heart condition. An arrhythmia or something."

"Maybe," Margie agreed, shrugging helplessly. "Or the bullet bounced around. I've heard of cases where it is actually carried in the bloodstream to somewhere else in the body where it causes problems... the lungs or the heart. A fragment of bullet or bone could have been carried somewhere else. Or just a blood clot, but I don't think there was even time for it to be a clot."

"Yeah. Something like that. They'll be able to tell on the autopsy. So what can you tell me about the shooter?"

Margie repeated what she had already told the dispatcher. She could only go so far in her description, considering the hoodie and ball cap and the speed of the chase. Cruz didn't write any of it down. He had probably already heard her description given to the dispatcher and would have caught any inconsistencies.

"How did he behave? Did he shout anything? Say her name? Did he act like he knew her?"

"It was too quick. I have no idea. He didn't shout or give any kind of warning. And there hadn't been any kind of disruption I had heard, so I don't think people knew he had a gun until he pulled it."

"Was Dr. Thorndyke his intended target?"

"I would say so, yes. She was the one standing at the podium. She started her speech and was promptly shot."

"There was no media here?" Cruz looked around.

There were now a couple of TV stations setting up their cameras on the sidewalk outside the park, since they wouldn't be allowed in. But they hadn't been taping when the shot had been fired. Margie guessed that no one had thought the opening a big enough deal to send a camera crew. There might have been a reporter or two with notepads and iPhones, but no one had expected the tragedy, or they would have been better prepared with all of the bells and whistles.

"How is your grandpa?" Cruz asked.

Margie looked over at Moushoom, who was patting Stella. He looked calm and serene while he waited for her. It would be a lot more sitting around waiting than they had planned for. They had counted on a half-hour or so of cere-mony shortly after they got there, followed by touring the gardens and then taking Moushoom back to his home, maybe with a stop at Peters' Drive-In on the way. Their fries weren't the same since they had changed their recipe, but they still had a million different milkshake flavors. Or at least thirty, which could be combined into countless varieties of milkshakes.

"He's doing just fine. I didn't expect to find him out of his wheelchair and up on the stage, that's for sure. But adrenaline, seeing that someone needed help... he just naturally went into action."

"Was he ever a medic? Maybe in the army?"

Margie shook her head. "No, not that he ever told me! But he's always been very quick in an emergency. And his grandmother was a well-known medicine woman, so he probably picked up some stuff from her."

"Well, it's too bad he lost this patient. It sounds like he did everything right."

"It wasn't because of anything he did wrong."

"No, I don't think so," Cruz agreed. "Whatever happened was outside his control."

CHAPTER FIVE

"*A*re you the police in charge?"

Margie focused on a young man approaching them. She nodded and stepped to the side slightly to include the man in their conversation.

He was a tall Black man, his skin several shades darker than Margie's. Slim build. His expression was anxious, eyes wide, his hands wringing as he approached them, looking like a child who had to approach a mean teacher with a question or a request to go to the washroom.

Margie tried to smile reassuringly.

"Hi. I'm Detective Patenaude. You can call me Detective Pat if you like. And this is Detective Cruz." She gave a little laugh. "He doesn't bite."

Cruz was solid, and he could certainly look stern and imposing when he wanted to. But Margie knew the other side of him. A tenderhearted family man, a Filipino immigrant who had definitely entered the police force because he wanted to help people, rather than being drawn in by the pull of having authority over them and carrying a powerful weapon.

Cruz could look friendly when he wanted to. He gave the young man a sympathetic smile. There was a lot going on here; a lot of people were going to be upset at what had happened, about the event being canceled, and myriad other little details that had just not gone right. It was upsetting to be caught in the middle of the investigation into a violent death.

"How can we help you?" Cruz asked.

"This is all…" the man flapped his hands at all of the controlled chaos going on around them. There were so many witnesses to be interviewed and people whose lives had been disrupted by the firing of one shot that morning. "I can't believe what is going on. This was going to be such a special event. And now…" He shook his head sadly.

Margie nodded, wondering what his part was in the opening. "Yes, you're right. It can be overwhelming. I didn't catch your name."

"Oh. It's Alan. Dr. Alan Pierce." He put his hand out automatically toward Margie. "I… work with Eliza. Or against her," a self-deprecating little laugh. "We didn't always see eye-to-eye. But I would never wish any harm to come to her." He hastened to make sure that they understood there were no hard feelings.

"Of course not. So, did you both work for the research institute together?"

"I had occasionally been contracted by the institute for one job or another. Running a study, doing research, writing up a paper for them."

"You knew each other pretty well?"

Pierce's wide eyes nearly popped out of his head. His hands were squeezing the life out of each other. "*Knew?*"

Margie hadn't realized her mistake. While she knew that Eliza had died, it wasn't yet widely known. Everyone would just think that she had been shot in the leg and was being treated at the hospital.

"Uh… I'm sorry, Dr. Pierce. I didn't mean to say that… but yes, Eliza died on the way to the hospital. I know this is a shock; I'm sorry to have to tell you."

"How could that be? She couldn't die just from being shot in the leg."

"Well, it does happen. Particularly with large blood loss. We're not sure yet exactly what happened. She seemed to have some kind of secondary reaction. I don't want to speculate on what happened before the medical examiner has had a chance to examine her and make an official report."

"But she was just here. I was talking to her yesterday. And then this… we were all so excited about the opening of the gardens. There was this big event to handle, and then we could go back to our research, to the science. But sharing something of what we do with the public, that was a big thing."

"I'm sure you both must have put a lot into the preparations. And now you don't even get to share it today. What are they planning to do? Have the opening in a few days? Will they keep the tents over the gardens in the meantime?"

"The gardens." Alan Pierce's hands came up to his mouth, still clenched together into a tight knot. "Oh, that's why I came to find you. You need to see what has happened." He looked back over his shoulder toward the tents.

Margie didn't know what she would do if there were another body in one of those tents.

"What is it?" she asked.

They started walking toward the tents, Pierce couldn't seem to find the words to explain to them what was going on. But he had said they needed to see, and he was taking them to the scene.

Margie turned around when she heard Stella barking.

The dog whined and strained to get to her when she saw Margie looking at her. She wasn't used to being left behind when Margie went for a walk in the park.

Moushoom shrugged at the disruption Stella was causing. "Why don't you take her with you?" he suggested.

"I don't think I can take her into the tents." Margie shook her head.

"I don't think it matters," Pierce said. "If you have her on a leash and under control. She looks like a well-behaved animal."

Margie wasn't sure how Pierce could tell, considering the noise that Stella was making. But she appreciated the comment.

"Are you sure you want me to take her?" Margie asked Moushoom. "You don't want her company?"

"I think she needs to be with you."

"Okay. I'll take her for a bit. We'll go have a look at whatever it is Dr. Pierce wants us to see. A little walk should settle her down."

He nodded and folded his hands in his lap as Margie untied the dog's leash from the wheelchair arm.

"Are you sure you don't want to go home? I can call a cab or Uber," Margie told him. "You don't have to sit around here. I'm going to be quite a while."

"I would rather sit in the sunshine enjoying the earth than sit in the stale air in my room and listen to the inane programming on the TV."

"Okay. But you tell me if you change your mind. Or if you get hungry or need something else."

"I have been taking care of myself since long before you were born," Moushoom reminded her.

"Yes, I know. But now it's my turn to help to take care of you. If you need anything, let me know."

He nodded. "I will tell you if I need something," he agreed. "Go, before the young man has a heart attack."

Margie scratched Stella's ears and turned back to Cruz and Pierce. Pierce did look like he was ready to have a heart attack. Or a meltdown.

"Okay, I'm ready to go. Family is very important to me," she said by way of explanation.

Pierce looked surprised that she felt the need to explain this. "Of course."

He led the way to the tents.

CHAPTER SIX

The humidity inside the tents was the first thing that Margie noticed. And then the heat. It was like a rainforest. Or what Margie imagined a rainforest to be like, having never actually been to one. She followed closely behind Pierce, Stella at her side and Cruz bringing up the rear.

"These aren't actually tropical plants," said Dr. Pierce, removing his glasses and wiping off condensation. "They are local species, for the most part. They will just be growing outside, subject to the vagaries of Calgary weather. It's just because they are covered and the sun is shining on the tent that it is so warm in here."

Margie looked at a little round garden ahead of her, bursting with color. "These are all local plants? Used to Calgary's environment?"

"Pretty much. We have some imports, but we try not to bring too much of anything non-native into an outdoor garden like this, in case it turns invasive. We don't want to be fighting another plant like creeping bellflower!"

He said it like it was something Margie should know all

about, even though she was not in any botanical circles. She shook her head. "What is creeping bellflower?"

"That is what we are fighting right now. You haven't seen the flyers or posters? We are posting about it on Facebook groups and other social media. People need to be aware that even though the little purple bells are pretty, you have to root it out of your gardens, yards, and back lanes. And you can't put it into the green bin. Black bin or burn it."

Margie blinked. "Why? What will it do?"

"It will choke out everything else. In a few years, it has gone from being nonexistent in Calgary to being in practically every yard."

"Purple bells?"

"Yes. I'm sure you've seen it. You can look it up on your phone. Creeping bellflower. But for now, we should go on."

Stella wanted to sniff everything. Margie had to keep her on a short leash to make sure she didn't touch anything she shouldn't.

When they drew up to the garden, Margie saw that there was something wrong. The pretty garden, while it looked fine from a distance, appeared to have been sabotaged. Flowers had been not just cut off like they would have been for blooms put into a vase, but someone had dug down into the rich black soil to remove a plant or several plants. Of those that remained behind, a number of them had been slashed, so they lay like colorful bits of confetti in the flower bed.

"Oh, dear. Do you know who did this?"

"No." Pierce's mouth twisted into a bitter grimace. "I have no idea who would do something like this. On opening day! We have worked so hard on these gardens. They are beautiful and practical, a testament to the hard work that everyone has done for the Institute and the park. A collaboration like this is hard to get. Using public space for our studies and beautifying the world at the same time... People come here to heal. Get some fresh air and sunshine. It has been proven that green spaces and things of beauty like these gardens lower your blood pressure, increase your endorphins, and provide many other benefits. They reduce stress and increase positive moods."

Margie nodded. "I know that they can be very beneficial," she agreed.

Stella pulled on the leash, wanting to smell everything in the small garden, to climb right in there and dig around where the soil had already been disturbed.

"Do you know when this happened?" Margie asked, trying to focus on the investigation and establish a timeline.

"I wasn't in here this morning, but other staff would have been. They would have said something if this had happened overnight."

"What kind of security do you have?"

"In here? Nothing. The tents are just to keep the gardens out of sight until they were unveiled. These plants were to be part of a public display. After today, anyone could walk up and look at or pick any of them. So there wasn't any security. Anyone could walk in. Someone might have asked them who they were, and they would have been asked to leave if they didn't have any business inside. But..." He shrugged and shook his head. "They would have had unfettered access to them tomorrow."

But whoever it was hadn't wanted to wait until tomorrow. They had wanted to make a statement. They had wanted to hurt someone. Just like the shooter.

"What do you think?" she murmured to Cruz. "Think this was related?"

"Had to be," Cruz agreed.

"Related?" Dr. Pierce repeated.

"To the attack on Dr. Thorndyke," Margie told him. "The chances that she was attacked and that the garden was torn up within hours of each other and are *not* related… it's just not very likely. We are looking at the same person or organization for both."

"Oh. I suppose so."

"Were these gardens shared, or was one person in charge of all of them, or…?" Margie trailed off.

"Each garden was different. They were for particular research projects, so the ownership of the bed and how it was managed depended on the project. Whose it was and what their purpose was. How they agreed to manage it."

"And this one is yours?"

"No… this one was Dr. Thorndyke's."

"Ah. So there is a close connection between the two events," Cruz observed, nodding.

"What was Dr. Thorndyke's project?" Margie asked, looking at the beautiful blossoms that had been destroyed. To her, it just looked like a garden. But to Dr. Thorndyke and whoever had savaged the plants, it had been more than that.

Pierce rubbed his chin, thinking about it. "I believe it had to do with medicinal uses of native plants. Probably with the goal of being able to patent them."

"You can patent plants?"

"You can patent the medicines you develop from them." Pierce looked like he wasn't finished, so Margie waited for him to think through what he would say. "You can patent plants you create—a new hybrid or genetically altered species. But Dr. Thorndyke was specifically looking at heirloom varieties. Plants that have remained stable genetically for many generations. Plants that might have existed in your ancestor's garden two hundred years ago."

Margie was reminded of Moushoom's comments about his kokum and her garden and kitchen. Margie might not know much about plants and medicine, but her ancestors had been medicine women, very knowledgeable in native plants and their uses.

Dr. Pierce pointed to her face, clearly referring to her heritage. "You probably have an ancestor who had these things in their garden. Are you from Calgary?"

"Manitoba."

He nodded. "Some of the same plants. And some different. And your ancestors may have traveled and traded with bands in this region. We don't know how far some of the bands traveled."

Margie knew she had ancestors who had come from many different parts of Canada. Each community had commerce with others. They weren't isolated from each other. Distance was a challenge but not a barrier.

"Was this the only garden that was touched? Or were they all damaged?"

"There was a little damage to some of the others." He pointed to the next one along in the tent. "That one is one of my projects, and a few blooms have been chopped off. But nothing like this. I think maybe the others were disturbed just to make it look like one particular garden hadn't been targeted." He looked down at it. "Even though it clearly was."

"It sure looks like it." Margie motioned to the hole that had been left behind. "What was supposed to be right there? Was something stolen?"

"I don't know enough about her project to know what's missing."

"I know," another voice contributed.

CHAPTER SEVEN

*T*hree heads turned to look at the source of the voice. A woman stood behind them, scowling. She was around Margie's age, her forehead permanently creased, with librarian glasses around her neck.

"Sarah," Pierce greeted. "Are you okay?"

"Yes, I'm perfectly fine," she told him in an acid voice, as if insulted that he had even dared to ask. Margie looked at the two of them curiously, wondering about the dynamic.

"Detectives, this is Sarah Kim. She works with Dr. Thorndyke. So this project is partially hers. Sarah… I don't remember the names of these detectives." He rubbed his cheek, embarrassed.

"Detective Pat and Detective Cruz," Margie said, pointing first to herself and then to Cruz. "How long have you been working with Dr. Thorndyke?"

Sarah pushed a long strand of hair back from her face. "Three years. I did some graduate work with her. Decided to stay on." She made a face. "*That* was a mistake."

"Oh? Why did you feel like it was a mistake?"

"I thought that we would be… colleagues. Equals. Yes, she has more experience and obviously she was my boss, but I still thought we would be on equal footing. Like… she would include my name on research papers I have worked on. She would put my name on the institute letterhead. I don't know. I thought I would be something other than just a glorified gopher. I thought the scut work would stop once I wasn't an intern anymore."

Her voice was full of resentment. Margie let her complaint sit by itself for a while, wondering whether she would reveal anything else. But the woman just shook her head, her expression stormy.

"If you didn't like how you were treated, why didn't you go somewhere else?" Cruz asked.

"Because what we were doing here was very specialized, and I wanted to see the results and be a part of it even if I didn't get my name on the paper. Though… I still hoped that I would get my name on it. If I went somewhere else, I would have to start all over again, washing the floors and answering email inquiries. I wanted to be *doing* the work."

Margie nodded her understanding. She pointed to the garden. "So… what was taken?"

Sarah looked at her for a few seconds without answering, as if she wanted to impress upon Margie how important she was to this investigation.

"It was *Aconitum napellus.*"

"And was there something special about… aconitum?"

"You haven't heard of it before?" Sarah needled. "Aconite? Monkshood? Wolfsbane?"

It clicked in. "That's poisonous," Margie remembered.

Sarah agreed. She folded her arms, looking at the small group. "Even poisons can be important when developing medicines. Sometimes, a large dose is poisonous, but a tiny dose can be very effective for treatment. Like foxglove."

"Digitalis," Cruz said promptly. "A heart medication."

Sarah pointed to him. "Bingo. You win the prize." She seemed to like him better than Margie. Maybe after working with Dr. Thorndyke, she had decided she didn't want to deal with professional women anymore. For a while. Until she had had some time to recover from the experience.

"Why would someone steal monkshood?" Cruz asked, tilting his head slightly at Sarah.

"And maybe just as importantly," Margie said. "Why was it here in the first place? Isn't that dangerous to have in a public display?"

"Well, not unless people eat it or rub it on themselves," Sarah said. "If they are going to do that, they deserve what they get."

"There is a children's playground and wading pool here," Margie pointed out. "Kids put things in their mouths. I would think that you really wouldn't want that liability."

"There were signs," Sarah dismissed. She looked down at the garden, where no signs were in evidence. "There were going to be signs."

"Were there signs and someone took them? Or did they ever arrive?" Margie asked.

"I don't know."

"Did you see them?"

"No."

"You were working closely with Dr. Thorndyke on this project and the opening. So were signs ordered? Were they delivered?"

"They were ordered. I don't know if they were delivered."

"They weren't placed in the garden," Margie pointed out.

"I guess not."

"Was everything supposed to be labeled? Or just the poisonous plants?"

"There were interpretive signs about the different kinds of

plants in the garden. We are still waiting for those; they'll be placed after the gardens are open. And there were small ones that you stick in the dirt to mark the aconite or to put any warnings on. You know, *don't pick the flowers* and stuff like that."

"Who would be able to recognize the aconite if it wasn't labeled?"

Sarah and Pierce looked at each other, and both shrugged.

"It isn't hard to recognize," Sarah said. "Anyone who wanted to could look it up online and then be able to recognize it. They are purple flowers that grow in these spires. The flowers themselves look like little hoods or helmets." She lifted her hands. "Anyone could pick them out."

"Are they hard to find? Would someone have to come here to find it, or would they be able to find it elsewhere?"

"It's a native species. Lots of people might have it in their gardens. You can order the seeds online."

"But if you wanted to poison someone, you would have to wait to grow them."

"The seeds are poisonous too."

"I think we're forgetting," Cruz said slowly, "Dr. Thorndyke wasn't poisoned. She was shot. We don't have any evidence of anyone being poisoned or stealing the aconite for its poison."

They all looked at each other, no one offering any alternate theories. Cruz turned to Margie. "We'll get the techs to get some pictures of the gardens and what happened here, too, in case it is related to the shooting. There seems to be a link. And now, you'd better get that dog out of here before she starts digging or something worse in the garden."

Margie looked down at Stella, who was still investigating the garden, pulling against the leash and sniffing the flower petal confetti. She wasn't misbehaving, just being curious.

"Can you smell who took the monkshood?" she asked in her special Stella voice, "Do you know who stole that plant away?" She indicated the hole where the monkshood had been. Stella sniffed diligently around the hole and the rest of the garden, but didn't miraculously begin tracking the thief.

Margie sighed. "Okay, I'll take her back to Moushoom and see who has arrived to help. We should get started on interviews soon, or people will leave. We'll need to talk to the two of you, too," she indicated Pierce and Sarah. "We need to talk to people close to Dr. Thorndyke and familiar with what she is working on."

"I'll be around," Sarah said, wrinkling her nose. "Am I allowed to start cleaning this up? If we are going to be opening to the public, it can't look like this."

"Not yet. You'll need to wait until someone tells you it is okay. The gardens are not opening today anyway, I'm afraid."

"We can't rent the tents indefinitely. They were only supposed to be here for a day so we could do the grand reveal. It costs money to keep them here."

"You will have to coordinate with the institute and the park to find out when the opening will be rescheduled for. I'm not in on that. All I can do is to ask you not to touch anything that might be evidence until we release the scene. It will only be a few hours. There is not much evidence to be collected."

Sarah sighed and rolled her eyes, but didn't argue about it.

"In the meantime, you can think about what we need to know about the work Dr. Thorndyke was doing and who might have resented her. Any enemies, relationships, any weird phone calls she might have gotten the past few weeks."

"You really think that whoever shot her would have called her on the phone first?" Sarah challenged.

"People do strange and unpredictable things. Whoever

had a bone to pick with Dr. Thorndyke might have called her to try to discuss it before attacking. They might have called to make threats or to complain about how badly done by they were. You weren't aware of any issues she was having?"

Sarah and Pierce looked at each other. Sarah shook her head. "Nothing unusual that I was aware of. Dr. Thorndyke was always fighting with someone. She wasn't easy to get along with. She was really... passionate about her work. And had definite ideas about how it should be done."

"I never knew botany was such a competitive field," Margie admitted. "I know botany is more than just gardening, but I have a hard time seeing people who spend their time with plants and growing things being anything but calm and serene."

"It's like any other science." The corners of Pierce's mouth quirked up into a smile. "Scientists are always in a race for the next big discovery. They want their names on this century's most important scientific discoveries. Whether they are in particle physics, recycling petrochemicals, or growing the source of the next big anticancer drug."

"Botanists are just as ambitious as any other scientists," Sarah agreed. "Some people can smile and get along while doing their job. Others... no matter what happens, they'll never be happy for more than a minute."

"And Dr. Thorndyke was more like the second type," Margie said.

"Yeah. She's done some really amazing things. She has had a lot of success and is really well-respected in the community. But she's not happy with that. She's the kind of person who will never be satisfied with what she accomplishes. She'll always think she should have done a better job. Gotten to the answer faster. Gotten the funding she needed a year ago."

"And she didn't play well with others," Cruz suggested.

Sarah laughed and nodded. "Yeah. Must have failed at sharing in kindergarten."

CHAPTER EIGHT

*W*hen they left the stifling hot tent, Margie returned Stella to Moushoom.

"How are things going out here?" she asked him.

"Settled down," he observed. "People are getting calmed down. But they don't want to have to stay here to talk."

Margie looked over the restless group and nodded. "We'll have to get them processed as quickly as possible."

A couple of vans pulled into the park, making their way slowly around the side of the chairs and the stage. They were unmarked, but Margie knew they were the techs and death investigator from the Office of the Chief Medical Examiner, there to gather any evidence they could from the shooting scene.

She waited until they stopped and then approached. She recognized Dr. Kahn from OCME and raised a hand in greeting. "Hi, Dr. Kahn."

"Ah, Detective Pat. Good to see you. I understand you were at the scene when the incident occurred."

"Yes. The victim was standing at the podium. She had just introduced herself and opened the ceremony. The was a gunshot, and I saw she had been shot in the thigh." Margie indicated the spot on her own leg. "I wasn't there when she was first treated; I went after the shooter. My grandfather did the first aid." She pointed to him sitting quietly in the wheelchair. "He bound it up tightly. When I saw her, she was sitting up and talking. There wasn't a lot of blood, and she looked strong and alert."

Dr. Kahn nodded as he listened to Margie's narrative and gazed around the site, stopping to look at the blood smeared on the stage.

"Not very much blood here at all."

"No. That's what I said to Detective Cruz. There isn't enough for her to have bled out. And she seemed okay. I don't understand how she could suddenly just go like that. She was talking, and then suddenly she wasn't breathing anymore."

Kahn grimaced. "I will talk to the paramedics and we will see what we can figure out in the postmortem. I can't tell you now what that might be. Sometimes there is a secondary condition. She might have had a heart attack. There may have been a second shot, but no one realized it. The bullet may have torn the femoral artery, and it was bleeding internally without anyone realizing it. A seizure or anaphylaxis. I won't have any answers for a while."

"I know. If it was something else, a preexisting medical condition, that doesn't stop us from being able to charge the shooter, does it? Because she wouldn't have died if she hadn't been shot."

"If a woman dies from being shot, it doesn't matter whether it was a heart attack or blood loss. It is still homicide."

Margie and Detective Cruz were tired, hot, and sweaty by the time mid-afternoon rolled around. Margie had drunk a couple of bottles of water, but hadn't had much else to sustain her through the day. Moushoom had finally consented to being returned to his air-conditioned room where he could nap and await further word from Margie about how the investigation was going. She was relieved to know that he was safe at home.

There wasn't much to be learned from the witnesses. They had seen even less than Margie had. Most of them had no idea where the shooter had been standing. Few had even seen Margie sprint off after him. In fact, one man had described the escaping shooter as being a Native woman dressed in much the same fashion as Margie, not even realizing the woman he described was standing right in front of him.

Margie was allowed into the building that housed the change rooms for the wading pool, even though it was closed. She used the facilities, splashed water on her face, took her hair down and quickly rebraided and twisted it up so that it looked smooth and neat again.

As refreshed as she could be, she returned to the field and looked around to see who still needed to be interviewed or what other tasks needed to be completed before the site could be released. She knew that authorities wouldn't like it if she kept access to the park restricted any longer than absolutely necessary.

"Excuse me, detective?"

Margie turned to find herself looking at Dr. Pierce once more. She steeled herself for the questions he would undoubtedly have about the progress of the investigation. He lifted a white paper bag and held it out toward her. Margie's hand closed around the offering before her brain had finished processing what it was.

Peters' Drive-In.

"I heard you talking about it earlier," Pierce said. "I knew you had been here all day and hadn't stopped for anything to eat."

Margie opened the bag to look at the contents. "Dr. Pierce, this is the nicest thing anyone has ever done for me. Thank you so much!"

He grinned widely. "I'm glad to help. I know you have been working hard with little to show for all of your work."

"Police work is like that sometimes," Margie admitted. "Would you like to share some fries while I take my break?"

"Sure."

They sat at a picnic table in the shade of one of the large pine trees, and Margie spread her meal out. The portions at Peters' were generous. She didn't know how hungry she was until the delicious, savory smells of her burger and fries started to tickle her nostrils. Then her stomach was growling, and she could hardly wait to take the first bite.

CHAPTER NINE

*M*argie had not anticipated the headlines in the news the next morning. She had assumed that not too many people would care about the death of a botanist from what should have been a non-fatal injury. It might get a little press, but it wasn't the kind of thing that grabbed people's attention.

Christina showed her the breaking news on her phone, holding it irritatingly close to Margie's face while she waited for her coffee to brew.

"Is this you?" Christina demanded.

Margie adjusted the position of the phone, drawing back, and looked at the series of rectangles with videos or cover photos.

Bizarre Murder in the Park
Police Stumped by Fleeing Shooter
Is the City Safe Anymore?

Margie pushed the phone back toward her daughter.

"Yes, I guess that is my case," she sighed. Though maybe if she was lucky it would be handed over to someone else. Margie herself had been at the scene and involved in the pursuit of the shooter and care of the victim. Her grandfather had given the victim first aid. Maybe she should be excluded from the investigation.

"You said you and Moushoom were at the park, but I didn't realize that you… saw it happen like that. You didn't tell me what happened," Christina pointed out.

"I didn't want to worry you. If I had, you might have been worried. You might not be able to sleep. I just… wanted to make sure you knew we were okay before you heard the story from someone else."

"I'm not okay if you don't tell me things. I want to know what's going on."

"Well, we were all okay. We were never in any real danger. It was just a long, tedious day."

"What happened to Moushoom's sash?"

Margie's head spun at the sudden change in direction of the conversation. Christina would have made a good interrogator. Never be predictable.

"What do you mean, what happened to it? He used it to treat the injured woman. To stop the bleeding."

"And then where did it go?" Christina asked insistently. "Did he get it back?"

"No. The victim was taken to the hospital with it still on. I can call them and find out what happened. Dr. Kahn at OCME will probably have it. Why, Christina? I don't understand what you are concerned about."

"That's Moushoom's sash. He needs it back. And we need to make sure that it gets cleaned so it doesn't have any blood on it."

"Yes, you're right. But I don't think it is urgent. I will follow up on it."

"What if they keep it and don't give it back?"

Margie knew that people sometimes focused on inconsequential things when their lives had been in danger.

Christina must be quite concerned about her Moushoom. Fastening on to the details about his sash was her way of dealing with the stress and uncertainty.

"If we can't get it back for some reason—and I don't see that being a problem—then I will see about getting him another one. He'll be okay until we can get that one back to him. Or a replacement."

"Do you know someone who makes them?"

"I know a few people I can ask, yes."

"Maybe *we* could make him a new one."

"We?" Margie repeated. "I'm not sure my skills are up to that level. I've done a little finger weaving, but I'm not proficient at it. I'm afraid... it would look like a kindergartner's gift."

"I could do it."

"You could," Margie agreed. "Do you know how to do it? We can ask someone to show you how."

"I was looking at videos online."

"Oh, that's a good idea."

"It doesn't look that hard. But I'll need some supplies."

"I can take you to Michaels later in the week. Make a list of what you need and we'll make a supply run."

Christina's shoulders lowered and her face fell into a more natural expression, finally relaxing.

"Can I do it even if you get his old one back?"

"Of course. I'm sure Moushoom would love it. You know how he loves you and anything you make. Especially your bannock."

"Well, he'd better not eat the sash!"

Margie giggled. She gave Christina a hug. The girl hadn't had a shower yet and smelled faintly of sweat.

CHAPTER TEN

*M*argie started her day at the office, glad to be able to sit down in the temperature-controlled environment, with coffee and water close at hand, after the long day at the park the previous day. It was a beautiful setting, but it had not exactly been the relaxing, regenerative day she would normally expect working close to nature. Instead, it had been frustrating and exhausting. She had woken up in the morning thinking she would just be having a pleasant time with her grandfather, but it had certainly not turned out that way.

"You're lucky you don't get sunburned," Detective Kaitlyn Jones observed, looking away from her computer to watch Margie settle in at her desk with a mug of coffee. "If I had spent all day in the sun, I would be covered with blisters."

Jones had fair skin and blond hair, and Margie knew from experience that she would burn in minutes if she hadn't put on a high-SPF sunblock. Margie tried to remember to put on sunblock during the summer, but she didn't always remember, and she didn't bother trying to get something over 25 SPF like Jones did.

"I wasn't in the sun the whole time. But you're right; it would not have been pleasant if I got burned doing interviews yesterday."

"What's on your list for today? Do you have anything identifying on the shooter?"

"Not yet. Canvassing for a street cam that might have caught him, but even if we did get him on camera, that will only give us directionality. Nothing is going to show his face, with the hoodie and ball cap on."

"Unless he took them off."

"Why would he take them off while he was still running? He didn't take them off until he was far away enough not to be observed."

Jones shrugged. "Sometimes they do. Change their appearance so you can't pick them out of a crowd."

"Yeah. I suppose we could get lucky, which is why we are canvassing, but I don't expect to find anything. I don't think we're going to identify the killer that way. We're going to need to find the motive. You don't just shoot someone in public without a pretty good reason."

"True," Jones agreed. "That's a big risk. I mean, standing up and shooting someone in full view of a hundred onlookers…"

Margie sipped her steaming coffee and navigated to her inbox, which looked too full and chaotic to manage, and then to the shared workspace for the investigation, which looked much more orderly and not so overwhelming.

"It was pretty crazy," she agreed. "If I wanted to get rid of someone, I certainly wouldn't want all those witnesses. Follow her home. Or wait until she is alone at work. I think she works by herself a lot."

"Maybe it is someone she works with, and that would be

too obvious. Everybody would know who it was or who was missing when it went down."

Margie thought that was a really good point. She jotted a note to herself on the notepad next to her keyboard.

"Or maybe it was personal. An ex-boyfriend?" Jones suggested.

"I think she would have recognized him. Even with a ball cap and hoodie, she would have known who had pulled the trigger. I don't think she recognized him. She would have said something. To Moushoom, or me, or the other people helping out. She would have said who it was. She wasn't killed right away. She was talking after it happened."

"That makes it harder to believe it was a coworker, too. She would have known if it was someone she worked with. Or wouldn't work with."

"Maybe. I think it would have been easier for a coworker to disguise himself than an ex. You are used to seeing people just one way..."

"But either way, you don't have many leads on the shooter."

"Not yet. Maybe we'll be lucky and there will be something on ballistics. Maybe it will match up to a previous crime."

Margie moused over the shared workspace, having a look around. "I'm hoping Dr. Kahn will have something helpful on the postmortem. He hasn't posted it yet."

"I'm sure he's just waiting by his phone, hoping to hear from you."

Margie grinned. She tapped the speed-dial button on her desk phone and picked up the receiver. It rang a few times before being answered.

"Detective Patenaude." It was Dr. Kahn's familiar, warm tones. "What took you so long?"

Margie was surprised. She clicked back on her inbox to

see whether he had sent her a preliminary report. "I didn't get a message from you," she said doubtfully.

"No, but I was expecting you to be harassing me about it long before this."

Margie chuckled. "Well, I had to get my coffee first."

"I'm afraid it won't be very enlightening when you get it. As we discussed yesterday, it was not blood loss that killed Dr. Thorndyke."

"Shock?" Margie suggested. "I know that can kill."

"Usually, we are talking about hypovolemic shock. Blood loss. There are other kinds of shock, but not many that would apply in this case. One of the possibilities is a heart attack, but unless she was known to have an arrhythmia, it would be unusual for someone her age. She had some occlusion in the arteries around her heart, like most of us, but nothing that I can see causing her death so quickly."

"So you don't know what caused her death?"

"I am still investigating. There was some unusual redness around the entry wound and the wound tract."

Margie frowned, staring at the phone. "What does that mean?"

"That is what I am trying to figure out. There was not a lot of time between the shot and her sudden respiratory collapse. But there was a few minutes."

"Yes," Margie agreed. "I chased the shooter, lost him, reported it to the dispatcher, and waited for the patrol cops. Talked to them, made sure that everything was on track with them, and got back to the park before the ambulance. Maybe... ten or fifteen minutes? I don't think it was any more than that."

"But long enough to start reacting to something."

"Do you mean... she had an allergic reaction? To what?"

"It's that inflammation around the entry wound," Kahn

repeated. "I think that the bullet must have left some kind of residue behind."

"Residue?"

"As if the bullet was coated with something," Kahn explained. "A foreign substance. I have seen something similar with old ammunition that hasn't been stored properly, and it has built up corrosion, moisture, maybe mold or bacteria over time, which is then transferred to the wound."

"So you think it was old ammunition that had been stored for a long time?"

"In this case, the bullet was shiny and new. Not old at all. But it would still appear there was something on the bullet that transferred to the wound and caused that inflammation and maybe had something to do with Dr. Thorndyke's collapse and death."

"What kind of something?"

"Something that killed her," Dr. Kahn said bluntly. "Something that was intended to kill her."

Margie's mind worked quickly, trying to pull all the clues and possibilities together.

"Something like monkshood?" she asked.

"Monkshood," Dr. Kahn repeated in surprise. "Aconite. Aconite delivered directly to the bloodstream could certainly cause death within that time. What made you think of that?"

"Because monkshood was stolen from one of the gardens. From Dr. Thorndyke's garden. Just that morning."

"Aah. Well, that is a definite possibility. I will request a rush tox screening for aconite. Thank you for the insight. That is very helpful."

"So you think that the bullet was somehow coated or smeared with monkshood before being loaded back into the magazine and fired."

"That's the idea."

Margie shook her head. "So he didn't need to get a kill

shot. He didn't need to worry about accuracy, other than actually hitting her. The bullet was not intended to kill her. It was just the delivery mechanism. He wanted to poison her."

"That would appear to be the case," Kahn agreed. "And it was most effective."

Margie thought back on her return to the park and review of Thorndyke's condition and the first aid that had been provided. Thorndyke had been talking, apparently in good condition despite the injury. The bleeding had been stopped. They only needed to wait for transportation. Then, there was a sudden change in the victim's condition. Complaints, vomiting, cessation of breathing.

It made sense as a poisoning. The initial period when they had simply treated the bleeding and she had been fine. Then, the poison had spread enough through her bloodstream to start causing symptoms and death.

"Thank *you*, doctor. That will help with our investigation."

Margie hung up the phone and stared at the computer, trying to structure the investigative procedure she would need to follow.

"What was that about?" Jones questioned curiously. "What's going on?"

"It looks like Dr. Thorndyke was poisoned."

"Poisoned? She was shot!"

"She was shot with a bullet that had been coated with poison. Maybe monkshood."

"What is monkshood?"

"A flowering plant. Very poisonous."

"Oh, I think I've heard of that before. Well, that changes the whole complexion of the murder, doesn't it?"

"It does," Margie agreed slowly. "The profile for a poisoner is very different from that of a shooter."

"But in this case, he was both."

"Or it was more than one person. One to doctor the bullet and one to shoot her."

"Maybe. You think it was someone she knew?"

"You don't see a lot of poisonings where the victim is random. The victim is usually well-known. Someone the killer lives with."

"Then I guess we need to learn more about Dr. Thorndyke and who she was close to."

"We?" Margie asked, straightening. "Are you free to give me a hand on this one?"

Jones had been putting a lot of time into another case, and when Cruz had been the one to meet Margie at Riley Park, she had assumed Jones would not be available.

"Sure. Going nowhere right now. I'll let it rest for a while and let my subconscious mind work on it. Maybe it will come up with something while I'm thinking about something else."

CHAPTER ELEVEN

*M*argie had taken down the information on the Hillhurst Botanical Research Institute the day before, knowing she would probably need to ask questions about Dr. Thorndyke's work if nothing popped in the witness interviews.

It would have been nice if the shooter had been careless and had turned up on their canvass of the neighborhood where Margie had lost him. It would have been nice if he had walked into any police station in the city and confessed what he had done. It would have been nice if someone on the police force had recognized him from a previous arrest, or he was picked up for a moving violation and recognized from the BOLO.

But the case had not solved itself while Margie slept, so she had to do something proactive.

She had suspected that the research institute would not be one of those big white research labs she had seen portrayed on TV. Or like the science lab in the high school she had attended. And she was right. They found themselves looking at a house that had been repurposed as a lab.

Margie checked the house number against the one in her notes.

"This is it, unless I wrote the number down wrong."

There was no sign or plaque at the front of the property showing that it was the institute they were looking for. But when they got right up to the door, a quarter-page piece of paper was taped to the door that confirmed it was the Hillhurst Botanical Research Institute. Deliveries were to be made to the back door, and nothing left in the view of the street. There was nothing that said the doorbell did not work or not to use it, so Margie pushed it firmly. She could hear it ring through the house.

It was a few minutes before there was any response. Then, eventually, there were footsteps, and the door swung open.

It was not Sarah Kim, but a younger woman, her lank hair brown and dull. She wore a dark shirt and pants with a stained white lab coat. She looked at Margie and Jones and didn't seem to know what to think of them.

"Who are you?"

Margie nodded curtly. "Calgary Police. Can we come in? We would like to talk to whoever is in charge."

She looked at them without expression.

"Can we come in, please?" Margie requested again.

The woman stepped back and looked around. Margie and Jones advanced, entering the house. The woman backed away a little more to give herself space. Jones closed the front door behind them.

"Great," Margie approved. One step done… "Are you the only one here?"

"I don't know." the young woman looked around as if she had been completely unaware of her surroundings until then. "What's going on?"

"You heard about Dr. Thorndyke's death?"

"I don't think there is anyone here."

"Do you work here? What is your name?" Margie had started off thinking that she was one of the scientists, but she seemed so clueless that Margie was revising her opinion. Someone's daughter, who obviously could not be left alone. Maybe someone else was there, or maybe they had gone out to run an errand, thinking she would be fine there on her own for a few minutes.

"Ramona." She rubbed her forehead. "Sorry, I was just... taking a nap. I don't usually do that here, but I couldn't sleep last night, and then after everything that has happened this morning, I just had to put my head down and close my eyes for a few minutes."

"Sorry, we didn't expect to wake anyone up at this time of day."

"No, I know, it's fine. I'm just... you caught me off guard, and I don't know what's going on." She squeezed her eyes closed and then opened them again wide, as if this might wake her up and clear her head.

"How about some coffee?" Margie suggested. "We can just have a wander around and see who is here while you wake up and get yourself together."

"I don't drink coffee." Big yawn. "It's very bad for you. You really shouldn't use the stuff."

"Well," Margie didn't want to get into an argument about the need for caffeine, so she avoided engaging. "Whatever it is you do to wake yourself up then. Grab a glass of cold water. Splash it on your face. Then you can tell us what's been going on today."

"Why don't you sit down," Ramona said, indicating a few chairs in the reception area that used to be someone's living room. "I'll go see who is here that might be able to help you. Usually, Eliza handles all of the public relations stuff."

Remembering how terse Dr. Thorndyke had been at the

preparation for the opening, Margie winced. If she was the most sociable person the Institute had, they were in trouble.

But she had also been the one who had approached them and made space for Moushoom, made sure that their people were included in the land acknowledgment, and been ready to give her welcome address and open up the gardens to the public. Those were all things that suggested she was good with people. Maybe the terseness had just been efficiency. Trying to get everything ready to go before the ceremony started.

Ramona yawned as she wandered out of the room. Margie and Jones circulated around the reception area, looking at the framed horticultural prints on the wall, a certificate of some sort, and a few potted plants arranged here and there throughout the room. Were they research studies too? Or just decorations?

CHAPTER TWELVE

*E*ventually, Ramona returned with Sarah Kim, and withdrew. Kim looked at them, faintly puzzled.

"Detective Pat?"

"Dr. Kim. We have some questions about Dr. Thorndyke and the Institute. It will take some time. Do you have a meeting room where we could sit down, maybe have an interview with each employee…"

"I don't know. Things are pretty disrupted right now. It really isn't a good time."

"Time is of the essence in an investigation like this. We need to get people while their memories are still fresh."

"I know, but it isn't a good time."

"What's going on?" Jones asked.

Sarah looked at her.

"Everyone keeps talking about what is going on today," Margie agreed, realizing it was true. "What *exactly* are you talking about?"

"There was… a burglary. We're still trying to get everything straightened out and inventoried. We won't know until then what is missing."

"A burglary. Did you call the police? I didn't see anything come in about it."

"No. We're just keeping it quiet. We don't want to make any waves."

"Don't want to make any waves?" Margie asked sharply. "We're investigating a murder here."

Sarah pulled back from her, shaking her head. "It was a burglary," she repeated. "I don't know yet whether anything valuable was taken. It might just be… mischief, or whatever you call it. There isn't any point in reporting it unless something of value was taken."

"What have you found so far?"

"It looks like…" Sarah swallowed and brushed a strand of hair back from her face. "Well… like maybe Dr. Thorndyke was the target of the burglary. Her project files, her research…" She sighed deeply. "I don't know where anything is."

"Ramona said that she's been busy all morning. Doing what?"

"Going through boxes. Like I said. Trying to inventory everything, Figure out what might be missing."

"I think you'd better show us," Margie said.

"We didn't want to make a big thing of it."

"Dr. Thorndyke was murdered yesterday. Today her research is stolen. It is a big deal. You can't make it *not* be a big thing."

Rolled eyes. "I could have if you hadn't shown up," Sarah muttered.

Margie and Jones met each other's eyes. What a piece of work.

"Do you want to show us?" Jones asked briskly, "Or should we just walk around and have a look on our own?"

"Is there any way I could *not*?" Sarah asked.

Margie considered. "Not really," she said. "This is an

investigation into a burglary of this building, related to a murder that took place yesterday. We have the right to see what was broken into. We are not going to go through your files, but it would be nice if you could tell us what you have discovered missing so far. Doing an inventory is good, but you will need to file a police report. Your insurer is going to require it. And whatever professional organizations you belong to will require you to uphold the law and be open about anything going on here."

"There is nothing 'going on here,'" Sarah insisted.

Margie said nothing. Sarah moved toward the stairs at the back of the house and they followed her.

"This is an invasion of our privacy," Sarah told them. "We have trade secrets. Confidential research results. All kinds of confidentiality issues…"

"We are not going to read your research," Margie repeated. "Can you show us the point of the break-in, please?"

Sarah didn't pause, but led them to the back of the house.

There wasn't a lot to see. The Institute had clearly not upgraded security when they had converted the house. There was a spring lock and a deadbolt. No electronic monitoring. The door frame had not been reinforced, and the door was hollow core. One shoulder blow was probably all it had taken to bust the door cleanly through the frame.

Margie looked around at the nearby kitchen windows. None of them appeared to have been broken. Just the door.

"Okay." Margie took a few pictures of the latch and the room with her phone. "And what room were items removed from?"

She tried to keep it general so that Sarah Kim would not feel the need to worry that she would demand the exact contents of the boxes or files. She wanted to see the room. That was all.

"This way," Sarah conceded, and led them up the stairs to a room that had once been a children's bedroom. Columns of four to five boxes were stacked along the wall. Some of them had been dumped out on the floor, the contents strewn around. Boxes had been ripped apart. Not just someone removing the lid and taking a few files. Someone had been angry. They had been looking for something specific and had been frustrated when they had not found what they were looking for. There was another stack of files and a handwritten list. Ramona had been going through the remaining files to identify what was missing and making careful notes.

"Tell me about the files that you know are missing."

"I told you they are confidential."

"I don't need to know what was in the files. I need to know how they relate to the murder."

"They are Dr. Thorndyke's files," Sarah said reluctantly. "All of these are Dr. Thorndyke's files."

"And what ties them together? Have you been able to identify any particular feature? A certain plant, or client, or some problem she was trying to solve?"

Sarah shook her head. "No. I don't know what it was. It looks… random."

"But he wasn't looking for just anything." Margie looked at the boxes. Not just Dr. Thorndyke's most recent projects. Not all of the files from any particular box. Just one here and one there. "The burglar was trying to find something specific."

"You don't know that."

"He didn't start at one end. He didn't go through the boxes methodically. He didn't dump everything or take something from each box. So what was he looking for?"

"I don't know."

"We would like to sit with you for a few minutes to

review Dr. Thorndyke's personal and professional life. Who might have had resentments toward her."

Sarah looked for a way to separate herself from the situation, but unlike with the confidential files or the junior employee who refused to be interviewed, she couldn't seem to find a reason to say no.

"Let's go back downstairs."

"Would you show us around first?" Margie asked. "I've never been to a botanical institute before; I'd like to see what it is like."

"It's nothing very exciting," Sarah said, but she had a smile on her face, and she led them out of the file storage room to give them a brief tour.

"I've never worked in a big lab," Sarah confided. "I've worked a few places in university and before coming here, but there aren't a lot of research institutes close by. I love this little place. Even if Dr. Thorndyke drove me crazy sometimes, I really think this is cute. And it still has everything we need."

CHAPTER THIRTEEN

*I*t was another children's bedroom, this one with work benches and walls lined with cupboards and open shelving, holding glassware, plant pots and supplies. There were a few plant specimens in jars along the windowsill.

Sarah took them to a microscope and selected a slide from a drawer full of carefully arranged samples. She put the slide on the deck, adjusted the eyepiece, and then stepped back for Margie and Jones to view it. Margie looked through it and was thrown back to high school biology, looking at a wall of rigid plant cells speckled with green dots of chloroplasts. She made an appreciative noise and stepped back to give Jones her turn.

"I remember this stuff from school," Jones said, echoing Margie's thoughts. "That's pretty cool."

"We have all kinds of slides," Sarah said, motioning to the drawer. "You could spend all day looking at different structures and tissues. It is fascinating."

Margie scanned through the labels on the slides to see what kind of order they were in.

"Do you have monkshood?"

Sarah frowned at her, then looked at the drawer. She fingered a couple of slides before pulling one out. Margie saw the nearly transparent purple petal mounted on the slide. Sarah positioned it for her, again checked the eyepiece, and then stepped aside. Margie saw that the sample was labeled *Aconitum napellus*, the name Pierce referred to it by. Aconite.

"Do you have a lot of samples of monkshood in the house? In the Institute, I mean," Margie asked.

"I don't know. Maybe a few. Why?"

"Do you have to do anything to handle it safely? I understand it is quite poisonous."

"A number of the plants we deal with are poisonous. There are protocols. Using gloves. Washing everything down afterward." Sarah shrugged. "It isn't like we're dealing with explosives or polonium or something. The necessary precautions are pretty basic."

"Do you keep track of all of your samples? Would you know if one of them had been stolen in the burglary?"

"Why would anyone steal aconite? It isn't rare or valuable."

"I'm just wondering. It was stolen from your garden in Riley Park."

"Well… yes. I don't know why that was done either. It seems like a pretty silly thing to steal. Like I say, it isn't rare or anything. You can grow it anywhere in Calgary. Order seeds on Amazon. I'm sure you can probably pick it up locally from a garden center."

"So there wouldn't be any reason for it to be stolen."

Sarah shook her head. "None that I can think of."

Margie nodded. Sarah led her on to another room. The master bedroom was set up as a multipurpose room. There was a boardroom table and chairs in the middle; the large closet at one end held racks of samples, all carefully packaged and labeled. There was a balcony, and the windows and balcony were both lined with rows of potted plants.

"You have really made use of the space," Margie observed.

"One of the nice things about working here is that even when you 'go to the office' you are surrounded with nature, inside and out." Sarah led them out to the balcony, and they looked down at the backyard, which was filled with greenhouses of different sizes and shapes.

"Were any of the greenhouses broken into?" Margie asked. "Was anything damaged other than the back door?"

"The greenhouses are not locked. Sometimes, we get broken panes; it's not unusual to have to replace some glass. Most of it is actually plastic. Sometimes we don't even know why it broke. Sometimes it is a baseball or a bird, or a rock kicked up in the back lane. Or just the weather and the changes in temperature. Like I said, we don't even know what did it half the time. Well, maybe ten percent of the time."

"So samples could be stolen from the greenhouses. Would you even notice it?"

"Not unless they were really obvious about it. If they did like they did in Riley Park and took whole plants and made a mess, we would notice. But if you just went in there and nipped off a shoot or a branch, one bloom or seed pod... no one would think anything of it, even if they noticed. We collect samples for cataloging or future studies."

Margie didn't know for sure what she was looking for. They already knew that Dr. Thorndyke had probably been poisoned by monkshood on the bullet, probably the monkshood that had been taken from the garden. There wasn't any need to look for another source. Unless the theft from the garden was misdirection, to disguise the real source or the real poison.

Sarah was looking at her, obviously wondering why Margie was asking the questions she was.

"Then there is the kitchen," she told Margie and Jones. "We use it as a sample prep area, indoor planting if the weather is not good outside, and break room, of course." She looked at her watch. "I really need to be getting back to work. So if that is everything…?"

"Did Dr. Thorndyke live alone? I know that officially, she did, but sometimes, people have partners who stay over some of the time even though they have their own place. Or there could be other circumstances. A grown child who returns home. A friend who crashes on the couch."

"No, I don't know of anyone who ever stayed over there. Eliza didn't ever say anything about it. But she didn't talk about her personal life. When we were here, it was business, and we were talking about plants. What studies were going well and which were not. Ideas for future work. Talk about staffing. I don't think I ever discussed boyfriends with Eliza. It would have been awkward."

"Some people talk about what is going on at home, or maybe challenges that were distracting them from the job. Or just venting, blowing off steam."

Sarah shrugged. "Like I said, I don't think I ever discussed anything like that with her."

"Would anyone else have? Who else is on staff here?"

"Right now? Just me and Ramona and… we have a couple of part-time students and researchers. They aren't here all the time, maybe a day or two each week. But they aren't here today."

"Do you think any of them know anything about the burglary?"

"Why would they?"

"Did you call everyone to tell them about Eliza yesterday?"

"No. It was all over the media today. I knew it was going to be. People called in as they heard. Or they didn't; they just talked to each other. It's just a small office; everybody knows everyone else. They call or text each other or comment on social media. Nobody here was *that old*." Sarah looked as though anyone Margie's or Dr. Thorndyke's age was ancient. "We all know how to reach each other quickly."

"Did anyone have any theories as to why Dr. Thorndyke was killed?"

"Not really. She could be a nasty witch sometimes. She was good at what she did and didn't put up with people who weren't. If you didn't know your stuff…"

"But no names came up when people found out she'd been shot?" Margie pressed, "Suggestions of people who might have done it or been happy that she was out of the way?"

"There are other scientists, people who work for other organizations. Or who only come here for certain projects. They tend to… not put up with her attitude either. Or with her trying to take all the credit."

"What about the other botanist who was at the park yesterday? Dr. Pierce. Did he and Dr. Thorndyke have any… outstanding issues?"

"They didn't like each other very much. But Dr. Pierce is a nice guy. I can't see him doing anything like that. I think it had to be someone… I don't know. Someone crazy. Someone who was just looking for someone to shoot. Not anyone we knew."

"You don't think she had ticked off anyone *that* much."

"No…"

"How did you feel about her? You weren't happy with her leaving your name off of papers. You wanted her to treat you as a partner instead of a student."

"So I shot her?" Sarah's voice rose incredulously. "Why

would I do that? I need references for my next job. It's pretty hard to get a recommendation from someone who is dead!"

Jones chuckled at that. Margie shook her head. "Yes, that could be difficult. But I'm sure you could get a recommendation from someone else you worked with on a project."

"But it's pretty tough if you don't have one from your current employer or who you interned with. They want to know why not."

"You would have—do have—a pretty good reason for not having one."

"Yeah, well, would you hire someone who didn't have any references but dead people?"

"People?" Margie repeated, wondering if there were more than one death on Sarah's resume.

"Just one person," Sarah said, rolling her eyes. "But I don't have much work history other than Eliza."

"How long has Ramona been working here?" Jones asked.

Sarah squinted at her, thinking. She shook her head. "Not very long. Why? Ramona didn't do anything either."

"Do you have evidence that she couldn't have?"

"She wasn't at Riley Park. She was here, holding down the fort."

"Alone?"

"Yes, because Eliza and I needed to be at the park. So Ramona was handling everything while we were gone."

"Was anyone else here with her? One of the part-time employees?"

"No, I don't think so. So she had to be here in case someone needed assistance."

"Do you know of anyone who made a delivery or came by while you were at the park? Who can confirm that she was here?"

"No. I don't know. I don't know why you're going on

about that. Ramona didn't have any reason to want to hurt Dr. Thorndyke. If you think she did it, you must suspect me too."

Margie looked at Jones, who raised her brows and didn't contradict Sarah. At least with Sarah, they knew she had been at the site. But Margie didn't think she was the fleeing figure in the hoodie. She couldn't swear that the shooter had been male, but she thought he had been.

"I didn't shoot anyone," Sarah said, shaking her head vigorously. "If you want to find someone who hated her that much…" Sarah cut herself off and shook her head one more time. "I don't know. I can't think of anyone who had it in for her. Anyone who would have wanted to kill her."

As the interview wound down, they naturally started to head back toward the front door.

"You'll give us a list of the files and records that are missing?" Margie asked. "We need that information if we are going to solve this case. We need to know the connection between the stolen files and Dr. Thorndyke's death."

Sarah shrugged. "I can't see a connection. I don't think one had anything to do with the other."

"But you'll give us a list?"

"Sure, of course."

CHAPTER FOURTEEN

"What do you think?" Jones asked as they drove back downtown.

Margie leaned back briefly and closed her eyes, relaxing while listening to the engine's hum.

"I think it was a good thing that we went over there. We wouldn't have known anything about the break-in if we hadn't. Why is Sarah Kim so intent on keeping it quiet?"

Jones tapped the steering wheel as she drove, thinking about it. "It could be that she's worried about the Institute's reputation. Doesn't want people to know they had such poor security, doesn't want to let them know about the research that might have been lost."

"But it would all be on the computer anyway, wouldn't it? I mean, even if you lose the paper copy, that's inconvenient, and it might be more comprehensive than the electronic file, but all of the study results would be logged electronically, and the study findings and final report would be on the computer. You might lose some working papers but wouldn't lose everything."

"Sounds right," Jones agreed. "If they're following standard practices. I can't see them losing everything just because someone broke in and took the paper copy."

"Maybe there is old stuff that isn't on the computers… maybe from a previous company?"

"Possible. I would expect that if Dr. Thorndyke had been allowed to take the paper files, she would have been allowed to take a copy of the electronic files with her, too. I guess some people aren't very technically proficient, but I would think that anyone her age would be able to manage copying files to a USB drive."

Margie called Dr. Pierce again and was able to reach him this time to confirm that he would be coming by to see her today to answer some questions. Like Sarah, he sounded perturbed that she would think he would have anything to do with Dr. Thorndyke's murder and said that he had told her everything relevant the day before.

Margie assured him they just needed to verify the facts and get his signature, and everything could be handled quickly.

Of course, that wouldn't be all they wanted once he got to the police station.

Once back at her computer, Margie looked for any updated files in the shared workspace for the case, but there wasn't anything new. No news that the suspect had been found and arrested. No tox screen back from Dr. Kahn. Of course, it was still too early for that.

She worked the other angles of the case while waiting for Dr. Pierce to arrive. Reading through the witness statements that had been transcribed, looking for patterns she hadn't noticed or anything that didn't fit. People never told the police everything. They would hold back because they didn't want to reveal personal information, they didn't realize what they had seen, or they had other biases that made them present their story one way without revealing certain relevant points.

Eventually, Dr. Pierce got there. He shook hands with Margie, looking somewhat anxious. Naturally, he wasn't thrilled about being there. No one ever wanted to be there, though there were those who got swept up in the excitement of being a part of the investigation of a major crime. It wasn't something that most of the populace had much experience with, so it was something to show off to their friends on social media. Even if it was for something tragic.

"How are you doing, doctor?" Margie asked Pierce. "I'm sure you're still reeling from everything that happened yesterday."

"Oh, I am, I am," he agreed. "I still can't believe that everything that happened was real. It could be a movie or a TV show... but not something that was actually part of my life."

"But you're okay?"

He seemed to consider and take stock for a moment, listening to his body and his emotions to see where he was on the spectrum.

"Yes, of course, I'm fine. I am not the one who was hurt. Killed. Eliza will be greatly missed by the community. We sometimes worked together on a project, but we were not great friends. I will continue to work... and my day-to-day life will not be affected by her loss. Not like her family members."

"Did you know anyone in her family? I understand she lived alone, and no will has been found yet among her possessions."

He shook his head slowly. "No. I just assumed that she had family. I don't actually know them."

Margie nodded and led him to an interview room. "This

shouldn't take very long. Thank you again for coming in. I really appreciate it."

"I just wish there was something I could say to help you. But it came as such a shock. I certainly wasn't expecting anything like this to happen to Eliza."

"No, I don't think anyone was," Margie agreed. "Except the killer, of course. Someone had planned it out carefully."

It might have been intended to look like a random, senseless shooting, but the burglary at the Institute proved that was not the case. It had been a targeted hit. Dr. Pierce was one of those people who had not been enamored with Dr. Thorndyke, and as such, he was on the suspect list.

They both sat down and got comfortable. Margie had left a bottle of water on the table for him and gestured to the coffee pot on the side cupboard.

"That coffee is fresh; please help yourself if you would like any. Why don't you tell me more about yourself and your relationship with Dr. Thorndyke? You mentioned yesterday that you sometimes worked together."

"Yes. There are not a lot of botanists in the city. You tend to run into the same people on various initiatives. Eliza—Dr. Thorndyke—had been around for a while, and so had I. So, of course, we had worked together."

"Was there one area of study that she was interested in? I don't really know what it was that she did. I was at the Institute today. A very charming little place. But I still don't know exactly what she was currently working on. It sounds like it was a competitive business, so you probably know a lot of what she was studying or bidding on. Were you working on anything together right now?"

"No, we didn't have any projects together right now, luckily." At Margie's questioning look, he hurried to explain. "I don't mean I am happy not to be working with her; I just think it would be difficult now. Whatever projects we were working on together would be disrupted. There would be a transition period while we figured out what to do."

"Right, of course."

"As far as the area she did the most work in or a pet subject… Dr. Thorndyke was mostly interested in developing medicines. That was her biggest area of expertise."

"Is that why she was studying monkshood?"

"I would assume so. Like Sarah said yesterday, many poisons have medicinal effects, if you can get the dosage right or extract the right compound safely. You have to be very careful working with such a toxic plant, but the results can be incredible. You can save countless lives. Improve people's quality of life."

"Do you know what the medicinal uses of monkshood might be? What exactly was she studying?"

"No, she knew how to keep her studies confidential. You learn how to keep a secret in this business. If you can't, no one is going to hire you. I haven't studied aconite myself, so I don't know what properties she might have been looking at."

Margie looked for another way to delve into what Pierce might know about Dr. Thorndyke and her business.

"What can you tell me about her history? The research projects she had done before? Her reputation in the community?"

Dr. Pierce pressed his lips together and didn't answer immediately. His eyes moved around the room, taking in the camera bubble in the ceiling and Margie's close attention. He had a sip of his water.

"Dr. Thorndyke… she was a good researcher. She was a competent scientist and knew what she was doing. She had participated in a lot of studies and always had something on the go."

Margie nodded encouragingly, hearing the "but" coming.

"There were… rumors," Pierce said tentatively.

"Rumors about what?"

"Hard to say. I can't tell you anything specific. But I can tell you... there were rumors that Eliza was involved in... controversial studies."

"Controversial?" Margie tried to think of what a scientist studying plants could possibly do that was controversial. Low bidding on a study? Buying stock in a company before selling them a patented compound that would change the face of their business? A cancer drug or even just something that promoted weight loss could be worth millions of dollars. Even billions.

"You might think that growing plants is a gentle business and that no one who does it could possibly be... cutthroat," Pierce said carefully. "But there was a lot of competition and a lot of... a lot of pressure to find the next greatest compound on earth. There are certain substances that, if they can be stabilized and patented, could change the world. Could change the lives of everyone who had been involved in their development as well as the people who need it." He echoed Margie's thoughts.

"And that kind of pressure could lead to controversial practices."

"Yes," Pierce agreed. "It could. One of those controversial practices was biopiracy."

CHAPTER FIFTEEN

"*B*iopiracy. I don't think I've ever heard of that before."

"You probably wouldn't, outside our industry," Pierce agreed.

He fidgeted and adjusted himself in his chair. Margie sensed that he would have been more comfortable pacing and lecturing. If he couldn't get out what he needed to while sitting, she might have to let him walk around to get comfortable enough to talk to her about it.

"Look, you are Indigenous," Pierce said abruptly, motioning to Margie's face.

She couldn't hide her heritage. It was as plain as the nose on her face. The very recognizable nose and other features, as well as her bronze skin tone, would never let her "pass" as white, as Christina's might. Christina's rounder nose and lighter skin made her less recognizably Indigenous. Her black hair could pass as Asian, Hispanic, or Italian. Her skin could just be sun-kissed.

But Margie herself was obviously one of Canada's original people. Her ethnicity had been clear even when wearing a mask that covered half her face during the COVID lockdown.

"Yes," she nodded at Pierce.

"Your ancestors used plants and herbs in their daily life. As their food and their medicine, as well as other practical uses. They knew how to treat a fever, nausea, pain. They knew what to give a fussy baby, a pregnant woman, an old man with cancer."

"Okay. Sure."

"They used plants in a way that we cannot replicate today. But we would like to. Many of their remedies did not have the side effects the drugs that we use today do, but were just as effective, or even more so."

Margie nodded. "They had a lot of experience working with nature instead of against it. They were a lot healthier than we are today with our lifestyle diseases." Margie touched her expanding waistline. "Mortality rate might have been higher because of childbirth complications and the lack of surgical interventions. But on the whole, they were pretty healthy before the arrival of the Europeans. At least if we are to believe the old stories."

Pierce shrugged. "From the descriptions we have from the diaries of early explorers and settlers, the Indigenous people they encountered were hale and hardy. What evidence we have in bones and other artifacts seem to bear that out."

"So... what does our old medicine have to do with this bioterrorism?"

"Biopiracy," Pierced corrected. "Totally different." He settled in more comfortably, a bit of the tension leaving his face and shoulders as he considered how explain it. "You may have heard of expeditions into the Amazon rainforest or other 'untouched' places to find cures for disease in the plants growing there."

"Sure. I thought it was kind of a cool idea. But I'm not

sure how it works. I'm sure they have to do more than just wander around in the forest looking for some plants they haven't seen before. And then what? Eating them? Testing them? What do you do, give it to a hundred people and see if anyone's symptoms improve?"

Pierce smiled. "That would be considered to be reckless and unethical behavior."

"Is that what Dr. Thorndyke was doing? Some kind of experiment using an untested plant from... the rainforest or something?"

"No. I'm only halfway there with my story."

"Oh, sorry."

"As you say, they could pick random plants and hope to be able to figure out what they were good for. They might run a bunch of tests and find out that it has compounds similar to foxglove, so they try to isolate them and see if they are effective in treating heart problems. They won't start with human studies, of course. They'll start with cells and tissue samples, then go on to animal studies, and eventually to human studies if they find something promising. But that still takes a lot of trial and error. There is a high failure rate. There has to be a better way."

Margie considered for only a second. Pierce had already planted it in her head. "The Indigenous people in the area probably already know the effects a lot of the plants have and how they can be used in medicine."

Pierce nodded his agreement. "So when they go on these expeditions, it is often with the intent of going to parts of the world where tribes have been isolated from modern society and still have a lot of traditional knowledge they haven't shared with anyone. That way, they can shortcut all of the initial testing and start off much closer to human trials."

"That makes sense."

"But *that* is not considered ethical in many circles. It is cultural appropriation."

Margie blinked. She knew the term, but to her, cultural appropriation meant white people taking traditional clothing, hair, or other styles from other cultures and passing them off as the next trend. Or people who had no roots in another culture claiming that they did. Or that they had a lot more than they really did. She didn't quite understand how learning medicine from another culture's elders qualified as cultural appropriation.

"How? They're not taking anything away from them and saying they developed it themselves. You can't very well go to the Amazon, come back with a new drug, and say they just came across it themselves."

"There has been enough of that kind of thing going on," Pierce admitted with a sigh. "But that isn't the only way to appropriate it. The question is who owns that knowledge. It is intellectual property, and modern society says that intellectual property has value."

"Well, I guess the members of the tribe own it, sort of. But doesn't Canadian law require a medicine to be patented to profit from it? I mean, we have patents, copyrights, trademarks, all of that kind of thing to protect it?"

"But that's *our* system," Pierce pointed to himself, "not *yours*."

"So it doesn't apply to Indigenous people?"

"What do you think?"

Margie frowned. "It seems like it should protect everyone."

"But is that how your people have protected their knowledge? With registrations and patent numbers?"

"No. It was a verbal tradition. Parents and grandparents passing it down from generation to generation. Medicine men and women sharing their knowledge with each other, teaching their children how to use it."

"Under the Canadian government system of registration, if you patent a drug made from, say, a geranium today, that patent will protect the drug for twenty years. So, by that measure, the protection of all of your traditional knowledge has already passed. Anyone can use it without consideration for the people who originally developed it."

Margie felt a lump in her stomach at the idea that their traditional knowledge could be discounted so easily, but she understood the principle Pierce was trying to impart.

"Okay. So if you or Dr. Thorndyke develop something new from an old Cree or Métis medicine plant, you can profit from it. You can protect your own invention of that drug for the next twenty years."

Pierce spread his hands apart, making it a question rather than a statement. "That is the way it works under our current capitalist structure. But the first principle of capitalism is that someone gets paid. Who got paid for that initial discovery?"

"Well… no one. That wasn't the kind of system that we followed."

"So if it was your ancestor's discovery, and they were not paid for it, then for me to use it without having to pay something is cultural appropriation. I am taking intellectual property from your people for my own use and profit without any consideration being given. What is its value?"

Margie raised her brows. "It could be millions. You hope it is."

"And shouldn't I pay you something for that? If your great-grandmother used it as medicine, and I develop a salable product from what you tell me, then shouldn't I pay you something for it?"

"Maybe a handful of beads and a good rifle," Margie said ironically. The way that the white man had paid Indians for their land and other valuable possessions in the past. Reparations were still being negotiated for some of those deals.

Pierce snorted. "You see the problem, then. Historically, we have not shown ourselves to be particularly fair in what we have paid for land rights, and that has been identified as a problem in today's society. And what have those expeditions paid to the Indigenous Amazonian tribes for the information they have been given about the medicinal nature of the plants that they use traditionally?"

"Probably nothing like what they were worth. Did they pay them anything at all?"

"We don't have compatible commerce systems. Our paper money, e-transfers, and Bitcoin don't mean anything to them. They may say they are happy to share their knowledge with their new friends, but you can bet they didn't understand that the scientists would harvest all of the plants they could find to use for medicine and leave nothing behind. Or that they would 'out' the tribe to make them targets for every other pirate looking for their own 'discovery' to sell."

"The same kind of exploitation that the European explorers and settlers perpetrated."

"And that modern society has said we would never repeat," Pierce said, putting his hand over his heart.

It was ironic that the man who was essentially apologizing to her for the past exploitation by the white European settlers was a Black man. His people had been exploited in other horrific ways.

Margie thought over what he had explained. "So *biopiracy*. That's what you're accusing Dr. Thorndyke of."

He held up his hands defensively. "I am not *accusing* Dr. Thorndyke of anything. I never have. And I've never worked with her on a project where I could have been accused of piracy. But there have been accusations made."

"Accusations that Dr. Thorndyke had engaged in biopiracy."

Pierce nodded.

"But Dr. Thorndyke wasn't on one of those expeditions that went to the Amazon or somewhere isolated," Margie guessed. The lump reasserted itself in her stomach. Dr. Pierce had already told her that Thorndyke had been focused on locally grown plants. Like monkshood.

"Right," Pierce agreed. "She never left Canada. Never left Alberta, as far as I know."

"So she has been looking for information on plants and their medicinal properties from Indigenous Alberta peoples."

"Exactly."

Margie thought of how solicitous Dr. Thorndyke had been with Moushoom when he had needed somewhere to sit, how she had asked him about his origins to make sure they were included in the land acknowledgment.

Acknowledging the native rights to the land on one hand while appropriating traditional knowledge from them on the other?

Was she that hypocritical? Or did she not believe she was doing anything wrong by seeking the traditional knowledge? If the elders did not realize the value of what they were sharing and thought they were simply being good neighbors, was Dr. Thorndyke guilty of something unethical or not?

"And there are no laws on this biopiracy?" Margie asked. It certainly wasn't something that her unit had investigated while she had been with them.

"There are no laws here to protect Indigenous intellectual property. Like you, most people have never heard of biopiracy or what is officially called 'a framework for access and benefit-sharing.'"

"So Thorndyke was not doing anything illegal."

"No. Potentially unethical. But nothing she could be

prosecuted for. And not something that most people would consider wrong. Asking someone for information without paying for it is not something most people would ever consider a problem. Especially Canadians, always so accommodating in helping others and answering their questions."

Margie jotted down a few notes in her notepad, her mind whirling through all of the possible impacts this could have on the case and the avenues they would need to investigate.

"If you didn't work on any studies that went in this direction with Dr. Thorndyke, then you probably don't know whether she'd had any pushback from the bands or elders she had gotten information from."

"Not directly. You would have to talk to them about that."

That was going to be an interesting conversation. And how many conversations would it be? She had seen the file boxes stacked in the storage room at the Institute. How long had Dr. Thorndyke been pursuing traditional herbal knowledge? And who had resented it?

"Do you know of any particular cases where Dr. Thorndyke had done this?"

"Only rumors. You would have to look at any patent filings she did or grants she had been given to see if you could track down any cases where she had used Indigenous knowledge for her own profit. Those are public records. But there may be dozens of other times that she has relied on traditional knowledge to direct her studies. It would be a huge task to audit all of her files and studies."

Especially since a bunch of them had been stolen from the Institute after her death. Knowing about the possibility of backlash, Thorndyke might have made handwritten notes of interviews that were never recorded in their digital files.

CHAPTER SIXTEEN

The next morning found Margie going back to the Institute once more. Knowing what she did now about Dr. Thorndyke's propensity for appropriating Indigenous knowledge about local plants and herbs, she was no longer fumbling around in the dark, hoping that someone would deign to let her know what was going on or happen to let it slip in their conversations.

It was Ramona who answered the door once again. This time, she did not look so sleepy and foggy. Margie gave her a friendly smile.

"Hi, Ramona. I have a few more questions for you and Sarah. I'm glad to find you both here today." Margie stepped forward and Ramona fell back, opening the door for her. Margie had learned over the years that being assertive and assuming that people would cooperate went a long way toward making it happen.

"Uh, Sarah is busy right now," Ramona protested. "She is in a meeting."

"Well, that's okay. I'll talk to you first. How long do you expect her to be?"

"I don't know." Ramona looked around nervously. "She could be... a few hours."

"Oh, well, if that is the case, we might have to interrupt her. But you and I can sit down for a cup of tea first."

"Okay..." Ramona led Margie to the kitchen in the back of the house, to the counter set up with tea service.

"Looks great. Why don't we sit down here." Margie motioned to the small table and chairs. She helped herself to the tea, and when it didn't look like Ramona was going to make herself a cup, she made the younger woman one too. They sat down at the table.

"So, do you have the file inventory ready for me?" Margie asked.

"What?"

"The inventory of the files that were stolen in the burglary. Sarah did tell you that I needed a copy, right?"

"Uh... she might have mentioned that. I don't remember. I'll have to get her permission."

"I'm sure she'll confirm that we need to know what was stolen in the burglary. A report has to be filed with the insurer and possibly with other parties, as well as the police. It's a big deal, them breaking in here and taking Dr. Thorndyke's files, even if it doesn't seem like it."

"It's kind of scary." Ramona lifted her cup to her mouth. "The Institute being broken into, I mean. I always thought I was safe here. Good neighborhood. We've never had trouble from anyone. I like working in this old house instead of an office building downtown or at the university. It has character, you know? And plants and flowers in every room..."

"It's homey. Comfortable."

"Yeah. But having someone just kick the door in, and march in here and take whatever he wanted to... I thought we had security cameras, locks, lots of ways to keep ourselves and the plants safe. But it turns out that the cameras weren't turned on. They weren't even real. Just a sham, to make people think it was secure. And the locks are only as secure as the latches, and they are just little short screws into wood."

"Was anything other than archived files stolen?" Margie asked. None of the stuff she had seen the day before had been locked up, or looked like it needed to be locked up.

"Uh… well, yes. Some plant samples. And a computer. The one that acts as our file server. We have to see what we can restore from backup."

"Sarah didn't mention that yesterday. So all of your systems are down."

"Yeah."

"And how could you inventory the missing files if you didn't have your computer systems? Did you have a hand-written record?"

"We kept a written log and then manually added it to the computer. It wasn't easy for me to find everything on the written log, because they weren't always archived in order."

"Do you want to get it for me now? Run a copy so you know that someone off-site has it too."

Ramona looked tempted for a moment, then shook her head. "I'd better wait until Sarah says."

"Do you keep files on the people you get complaints from?"

Ramona's eyes widened. "Complaints?"

"You must have gotten some complaints. People who felt like Dr. Thorndyke had taken advantage of them. People who thought they deserved a part of what she made based on what they had told her."

"I don't know what you're talking about."

"You must have heard complaints." Margie rolled her eyes. "You can't tell me that every call you get through on the main number is from someone who is happy."

"Well… no," Ramona admitted.

"And you're not supposed to keep track of anyone who made complaints? For a blacklist? People to block or that Dr. Thorndyke wasn't here for?"

"I don't know. I would give the messages to Sarah, but she didn't say what she did with them, and I never saw a list of people I shouldn't talk to."

"You just had to remember for yourself?"

"I guess, yeah."

"I'll have to ask Sarah for that, then. I'm sure there must have been a list kept."

"I guess she would know."

"What else was stolen? Other than the files and the computer?"

"Some plants and samples..."

"Like what?"

"Uh... lily of the valley, castor bean, wild rose hips, sweetgrass... fireweed. I don't remember all of them."

Margie knew several of the plants mentioned were poisonous or had medicinal properties. Moushoom would know more about them. Margie had been trying to learn more of the plant lore he knew, but she hadn't gotten very far in her studies. She was always busy with other things and didn't spend enough time with Moushoom to get all of the old knowledge firmly implanted in her brain.

She needed to address that shortcoming.

In the meantime, she wrote down the plants that Ramona had mentioned. She could ask Moushoom about those ones in particular. And see what he knew about monkshood, besides that it was poisonous.

"Had many people complained about Dr. Thorndyke's biopiracy?" she asked Ramona conversationally.

Ramona looked at her, startled. Her eyes widened, and she took a couple of gulps of the hot tea, which brought tears to the corners of her eyes.

"What are you talking about?"

"You know what biopiracy is."

"Dr. Thorndyke said it was a lot of bunk. No one owned the rights to those plants, just because they had been used in traditional medicines. She said that the Indians—" her eyes flashed to Margie's face, "that the First Nations couldn't own all of the knowledge about those plants. It was just them... trying to get more free handouts. Money just for being born in a certain genetic line instead of white."

Ramona dropped her eyes to the table and her fingers tightened on her cup.

"She said they were always just trying to get money they hadn't earned. She wasn't trying to make money off of their backs; they were trying to make it off of hers."

And that opinion was unlikely to make Dr. Thorndyke very popular if she repeated it outside the walls of the Institute, but her attitude had undoubtedly been obvious to the people she had worked with. Pierce had been aware of it. He had heard it from other people in the community.

"So who complained about it? If Dr. Thorndyke had talked about this entitled attitude, it must have been in response to something. Someone had made complaints about her or complained to her about the way she was using traditional knowledge for profit."

CHAPTER SEVENTEEN

*U*nsurprisingly, Sarah had been even less forthcoming than Ramona. Margie had felt from the start that Sarah was keeping things from her. She didn't know whether it was just because she had problems with authority or if she was protecting herself. Or some other reason Margie hadn't thought of.

She spent a frustrating day trying to chase down the information the Institute was not cooperating on. Who Dr. Thorndyke had been working with. Who had been upset. Who had been consulted in the first place.

Margie dug through the social media posts of not just Dr. Thorndyke, but everyone associated with the Institute at one point or another. Which was a lot of people. Margie tried to map everyone out, but especially those in the Indigenous communities. She recognized some of the names, mostly of chiefs or others who were in the administration of the bands. She hadn't had much to do with anyone other than her family in Calgary. She would have known more of the names back in Manitoba. And relationships could be complicated within the Indigenous community, with multiple connections between individuals and families.

At the end of the day, she was happy to go home to her own family. Christina was going to a movie with Tracy, so Margie decided to visit Moushoom in the care center. She took Stella with her, as usual. Stella knew the way there and knew the routine once she got there, greeting and spending time with those in the common area on the main floor before taking the elevator up to see Moushoom.

Margie tapped on the door, but Moushoom was dozing in front of the TV and didn't rouse until she entered the room and spoke to him, gently nudging his arm until he woke up. He blinked at her and gave her and Stella a big grin. "There you are, daughter. I have been wondering how the investigation was going."

"Oh, I guess you probably have." Margie sat down on the end of the bed to be at the same level as her grandfather. "I've been spinning my wheels a bit, actually. I'm getting closer, but tracking down the necessary information is not as easy as I would like!"

Moushoom nodded, his eyes sparkling with interest. "Do you know who did it yet? Who it was that shot at her?"

"Not yet. But I think it was someone who was angry with her for the way she had gone about her research." Margie explained how Dr. Thorndyke had talked to Indigenous elders to find out what she could about the medical knowledge they had of the various plants and herbs around them in order to exploit it.

Moushoom rubbed his whiskery chin, thinking about that.

"We have always been happy to share our knowledge to help out brothers and sisters," he said. "We are all blessed by this wisdom when it is shared." He pressed his lips together, thinking about the way that the knowledge would then be used. "But for her to sell that wisdom for money... I can see why people would not be happy about this."

Margie nodded. "I've reached out to a few people today to try to find those that Dr. Thorndyke talked to. But on the other hand... I don't want it to be one of our people."

"No, of course not," Moushoom agreed. "But you need to find out where the trail leads. You are sworn to find the truth and pursue justice."

"Yeah, I know."

Margie's phone rang. She slid it out to look at the screen, and nearly put it back away without answering it, then changed her mind. It wasn't the emergency dispatcher number she was familiar with, but it did say Emergency Services.

"Detective Pat."

"Oh, Detective," the voice was young, a little excitable, not someone who spoke to the police regularly. "You don't know me, but we did meet. At Riley Park. My name is Bob. I was just calling because I have your grandfather's scarf. The one he used to tie up that woman's bullet wound."

"Oh, his sash," Margie corrected, looking at Moushoom and smiling.

"Sash, of course, I'm sorry. I would like to be able to return it to him. I saw your name in the paper. I hope you don't mind me tracking you down like this. But I didn't want it to be thrown out. It looked... it looked like it was something that was important to him."

"Yes, it is," Margie agreed. "Thank you. Do you want me to pick it up from somewhere? The hospital?"

"No, I'm heading out the door to run some errands. I thought I could bring it to you while I'm out. Where are you?"

"You really don't need to do that. I can pick it up sometime. You don't need to drive all over the city to see me."

"I'm going to be out anyway," Bob assured her, "and I am already driving all over the city. That was why I thought it would be a good time to drop it off to you. I'm bound to be going your direction for something else."

"Really? Well, that's very kind of you. I'm near Seventeenth Avenue Southeast, International Avenue…"

"Yeah, I was going to hit East Hills Costco. That's not far from you."

"No, it's not a bad drive," Margie admitted. "Hang on a second while I check the address. I'm at my grandfather's right now, and I don't actually know the street address."

She lowered the phone and looked around the room to see if the address was noted beside Moushoom's phone or if she would have to pull it up on Google. She saw the fire evacuation plan beside the door, and leaned close to look at it. "Yeah, here it is…" she relayed the address to Bob. "Just give me a call when you get here, and I'll come down to get it."

"Great, thank you for your help, Detective. I'll see you soon."

Margie ended the call and turned back to Moushoom, smiling. "That is the person who has your sash and is going to bring it by."

"Oh, good." Moushoom fingered the place the sash was usually tied around his body. "I have missed it. Usually, the only time I don't have it on is when it is being washed."

"I know." Margie sat back down again. "When we were at Riley Park. You were telling me about your Kokum and her garden."

Moushoom nodded. His eyes were dreamy and far away. "It was a very peaceful place. There was always lots of work to be done, but it wasn't stressful. It was always interesting. Kokum always had many stories, and they helped me to remember what to do and what the different plants were good for. What parts could be used and how to handle them safely."

Margie nodded. "Because some of them are poisonous to touch. You wouldn't want to get them on your skin."

"Yes. The more powerful the medicine, the more careful you have to be of how you handle the plant."

"The poisonous ones were the ones with the most powerful medicinal properties," Margie rephrased.

Moushoom nodded. "Yes."

"Did she have monkshood in her garden?"

"We called it wolfsbane."

"Right. What did she use wolfsbane for?"

"The warriors sometimes used it to tip their arrows. Or to poison predators who roamed too close to the village. Wolves or other animals. There is a reason it is called wolfsbane."

"And that's the only thing you used it for?" Margie was disappointed. She had been hoping to learn more about how it could be used. What Dr. Thorndyke might have been planning to use it for.

"It could be used for visions," Moushoom told her. "She said it made you feel as if you were flying. But it had to be prepared the right way. Too much, and it could stop your heart."

"How did your Kokum know how to prepare it?"

He shrugged. "Her Moushoom was a powerful medicine man. And his ancestors before him. It was passed down from generation to generation. But now… no one seeks visions anymore. They look it up on Google."

Margie chuckled. "Until something new comes along to replace it. I'm sorry to see the old knowledge being lost. Do you know how to prepare monkshood—wolfsbane, I mean?"

He looked at her thoughtfully. Then he closed his eyes, thinking about it. "I am not sure I remember everything. I would have to remember everything to do it the right way. If

I did it all from start to finish, I would remember. But just talking… I might miss something."

Margie pictured herself and Christina with Moushoom in their kitchen, brewing up a pot of wolfsbane on the stove. She wasn't sure that was such a good idea.

Hopefully, there were others, like Moushoom, who still had the traditional knowledge to pass down or write down for others.

"What about these other plants?" Margie asked, pulling out her notebook to find the page. "Lily of the valley, castor bean, wild rose hips, sweetgrass, and fireweed."

"Lily of the Valley is a heart remedy. Like foxglove. Castor bean has many benefits. It helps with healing wounds and childbirth." He cocked his head. "But both have to be prepared properly. Like wolfsbane."

"They are poisonous."

"They can be harmful or helpful."

"Castor bean—that's what they make ricin from, isn't it?"

She didn't expect Moushoom to know, but he nodded his agreement. "Many medicine plants can be harmful if used the wrong way."

Margie shuddered.

"But others are not so dangerous," Moushoom assured her. "Rose hips, sweetgrass, fireweed, you can use those without harm. I know you are familiar with sweetgrass."

"For smudging, yes." Margie nodded. She had participated in sweetgrass ceremonies in the past. And had drunk rose hip tea without ill effect.

But the thought of what Dr. Thorndyke's killer might plan to do with Lily of the Valley or castor beans was chilling.

CHAPTER EIGHTEEN

*H*er phone rang again. She looked down at it. Again, it said Emergency Services. Her Good Samaritan must not have been able to get away from the hospital as he had hoped. She answered the call.

"Hello?"

"Detective Pat. It's Bob. I am here. Just in the lobby waiting for you."

"Oh, great! I'll be right down."

Margie headed toward the door. "I'll be right back, Moushoom."

Stella galloped after her. Margie laughed. "You just stay here with Moushoom, girl. I'll be right back."

But the dog would not be deterred. They had never left her alone with Moushoom, and Stella was sure Margie was going to go home and abandon her there. Not that it would have been a bad thing for her. Moushoom and the staff would have spoiled her to bits.

Margie relented and just let Stella come with her. She would just be grabbing the sash and returning to

Moushoom's room. Stella wouldn't get into any trouble coming along with her.

She rode the elevator down to the lobby. There she saw a slimly built young man waiting for her with Moushoom's sash in his hands. Bob was wearing a medical mask and gloves. His eyes crinkled as he smiled and nodded. Margie approached him. "Thank you so much. It was very kind of you to come all this way to return it."

She could see that the sash had been laundered. It was not soaked or stained with blood. Margie reached out a hand to receive it.

Stella growled and snapped at Bob, making him jerk back in alarm. Margie spoke sharply to Stella, irritated. "Hey, you don't behave like that! Why would you act like that when someone is giving Moushoom's property back?"

Bob stood there, his hand out, not sure what to do. Margie couldn't blame him. An unknown dog could react unpredictably, and before he knew it, he might have a slash down his arm. Then they would have to use the sash again. And get it laundered a second time.

Bob had a Calgary Parks polo shirt on. Margie frowned, trying to reconcile this in her mind. His caller ID had said Emergency Services, and she had assumed that he was one of the paramedics calling from the hospital. When he had called a second time and she had realized he was on his cell phone, she had wondered about it briefly, but the moment of doubt had been wiped away by her relief at getting Moushoom's sash back.

But if he was from Calgary Parks, why was he calling from a phone routed through Emergency Services?

"Who are you, again?"

"We met at Riley Park," Bob told her with a smile. "I was helping out with the arrangements there. I went with Dr. Thorndyke to the hospital, that's how I ended up with the sash. And I wanted to make sure that got back to your grandfather."

He thrust it towards her again, and Margie nearly took it from him. But Stella pushed between them, barking at Bob and driving him back. Margie looked at the sash, looked at the hand holding it.

A gloved hand.

Why was he wearing gloves? Why was he pretending to be one of the medical professionals? Or if he was a medical professional, why was he pretending to be with Calgary Parks?

"Who are you?" she demanded.

She sized him up. A slimly built male, light-skinned, around six feet tall, just as she had described the shooter to the dispatcher the day of the shooting. It had been impossible to see his face, and he now had most of his face covered by the mask. She couldn't be sure. But it could have been him.

Bob apparently decided that this meeting wasn't working out as planned. He took a step back, looking at Stella, looking at Margie, taking another step.

"You'd better hold it right there," Margie told him. "Put your hands up. Identify yourself."

"You don't understand," Bob growled. "I brought this back to you. I am not the bad guy here. I wanted to do something for you and your grandfather. Just take the sash —" He held it out to her, and Stella decided she'd had enough. She launched herself at the stranger, her jaw clamping down on his forearm.

Bob let out a yell and tried to shake her loose. The sash fell from his grip to the floor. Someone watching let out a shriek of alarm.

"Get down on the ground!" Margie ordered. "Hands behind your head!"

He didn't want to do it. He had other plans. But with the dog hanging off his arm and the sash on the floor, he could no longer attack or escape. Margie hoped he didn't have his gun on him. If he chose to use his non-dominant hand to fire, it could be messy. Hopefully, he had ditched it after shooting Dr. Thorndyke.

There was a moment of hesitation, and then the man obeyed, lowering himself to his knees and then to the floor. Margie pinned him down and pulled his arms behind his back. "Let him go, Stella. Let go."

Stella had never had any K9 training. But they had played ball with her hundreds of time, often having to tell her to let go of the ball if they were to throw it for her again. Stella rolled her eyes toward Margie. It took her a few seconds to decide that Margie was no longer in danger, and she eventually released the stranger's arm.

Bob was arguing, protesting Margie's treatment, still saying he was just trying to do something nice for her. She ignored him, holding his hands together behind his back with one hand and patting him down with the other.

He did have a gun. Margie removed it and pushed it away, out of his reach.

"Call 9-1-1," she told the receptionist, who was staring at her with wide eyes and an open mouth. "Officer in need of assistance. Suspect in custody."

It took the woman a minute to move, but eventually, she did. She called the emergency number and relayed the message. It was a few long minutes before a patrol car pulled up to the building, siren wailing. Getting a fire engine or ambulance would have been faster; the fire station was only a block away.

A couple of officers hurried in.

"Detective Patenaude," Margie introduced herself. "Off-duty. Here, if you could take him. He was armed and could still have another weapon on him. I could not do a full search."

She transferred custody to the two officers. "He might need medical attention. My dog bit him."

They sorted him out. Bob did not have a second gun, but did have puncture wounds in his arm that would need to be taken care of at the hospital.

One of the cops reached for the sash. "Is this yours?"

"Don't touch it," Margie snapped.

He froze with his hand stretched out toward it.

"Gloves," Margie ordered. "It is evidence. I don't know what he's done… but it may be contaminated with a toxic substance."

The cop looked green. He agreed that gloves would be a good idea, and after putting them on, he picked the sash up carefully to transfer to a large paper evidence bag.

"Now, do you want to tell us what this is all about?" the senior partner demanded. "I think we need the whole story now. And your identification, please."

Margie pulled out her wallet and presented both her operator's license and her police identification. "I believe this may be the Riley Park shooter," she told them. "At any rate, he's carrying a gun, so book him on that, and I'll catch up with the rest. With any luck, the ballistics will match with the bullet that killed Dr. Thorndyke."

She transferred her attention to the man. "So who are you, really?"

Bob's face contorted with anger. "You have no idea what Dr. Thorndyke was doing. You, of all people, should understand what she was up to, stealing from the First Nations. Using their knowledge accumulated from generations of medicine men and women for her own profit!"

"But who are you? Are *you* indigenous? I don't understand why you would get involved in something like this."

"The knowledge needs to be protected! Your people need to be protected from—"

"Let me get this straight. You're not even Indigenous, and you're willing to step into the middle of this issue with weapons to *kill*. Not just Dr. Thorndyke, but *me* and my grandfather!"

"I wasn't going to—"

"You weren't? What are we going to find when we have that sash tested? Wolfsbane? Or is it ricin this time? Something else from the samples you stole from the Institute?"

Bob's eyes burned. "You don't understand."

"No," Margie said flatly. "If I understood, I would be crazy. Like you."

"I am protecting your way of life. I am protecting traditional knowledge. Keeping people like Dr. Thorndyke from stealing it right out from under your noses. You don't even know the value of what you own!"

"The knowledge is priceless," Margie retorted. "Nobody can change its value. Not Dr. Thorndyke and not you. It has served generations of my ancestors, and maybe it will continue after me and my daughter too. But whether it does or not... it isn't *yours* to take or to defend. The wisdom of our elders doesn't belong to anyone else."

"That's what I'm trying to say. I talked to your grandfather that day. He is very generous and open. He should be honored for that."

"You don't honor a man by trying to kill him and his daughter. Or by killing anyone else." Margie shook her head and started to walk away from him. She turned back. "When did you talk to him? Before or after you killed that woman?"

"It was after she was killed," Bob said after a moment of consideration, his eyes narrowing. Maybe he realized now that he needed to be careful how much he said, each confession piling another year on to his sentence. "While you were off in the tents with the other scientists."

"So you killed her, ran away from me, and then came back to sit there and chat with my grandfather while everyone looked for you and interviewed witnesses?"

Bob gave her a little smile and shrugged. "I was right there under your noses. Wearing my shirt." He looked down at the Calgary Parks logo on the blue polo shirt that had made him blend in with the rest of the staff.

He'd been right there while everyone had been looking for him. Sitting there proudly like the cat that got the cream.

And then he had been brazen enough to go to the hospital to somehow get his hands on Moushoom's sash. Maybe he really was with Emergency Services or some kind of medical professional or staff with access at the hospital.

Margie let her breath out slowly, petting Stella to calm herself.

CHAPTER NINETEEN

*O*nce everything was settled down again, Margie returned to Moushoom's room and found him sitting near the window rather than in front of the TV, looking down at the flashing lights of the emergency vehicles below.

He turned his head to face her.

"Oh, you did not forget about this old man," he said, giving her a little smile. "I thought that with all the excitement, you might have forgotten why you were here."

"No. I just had to make sure everybody knew what they were doing. Get them all squared away."

He didn't ask her what had happened and why the police and ambulance were there. He looked at her hands. "My sash?"

"No…" Margie looked down at her empty hands as well. "Unfortunately… something got spilled on it." She looked at his face. "I don't know how long it will be before you can get it back."

If it had been poisoned, it would be evidence in the

shooter's trial. And it might take several years before he was convicted and all avenues of appeal exhausted.

"We will need to get you another one."

Moushoom nodded. He was studying her face. She wondered how much of what had happened he could read there. She decided not to tell him unless he asked. He didn't need to know that the killer had sat next to him and talked to him. That he had justified what he had done by saying he was protecting their rights and their generational wisdom.

Christina called to find out where Margie was after returning home to find a dark and empty house. She had Tracy drop her off at the nursing home so she could also pop in for a visit.

Margie knew it was getting late and Moushoom should be in bed asleep. Normally, a nurse would have been around already to tell them to say their goodbyes so that Moushoom could get the rest he needed. But today, after the disruption and what had happened in the lobby, they appeared to have decided to leave her alone and let her figure out how to handle everything.

Christina opened the door quietly and tiptoed in. "It is so quiet out there," she whispered. "I'm afraid I'm going to wake everyone up."

Moushoom smiled and got a hug from his favorite great-granddaughter.

"I didn't expect you to be back so early," Margie told Christina. "I thought you would be out for a couple more hours."

"After the movie... I just didn't feel like going anywhere else. I felt like I needed to be at home. With you." She looked at Moushoom. "And with Moushoom."

"Well, I'm glad you came home early. Moushoom and I were just talking about his sash. Remember how you and I were talking about how we would need to get a new one?"

Christina laughed. "Yes," she agreed, and dug into her purse.

"I know you were thinking about learning how to do it yourself, but we haven't had the chance to get to the craft store yet..."

Margie watched in wonder as Christina pulled a long piece of woven material out of her bag, letting it unfold as she did so.

Moushoom made an excited sound. "What is this? What did you do?"

Christina took it over to him, and kneeling in front of his wheelchair, tied it gently around him. She ran a thumb over the weaving. "It isn't as nice as your last one. It's sort of uneven. As I do more, I'll learn how to keep it more consistent. This was my first try."

"It is lovely!" Moushoom ran his fingers over it. "It is my favorite sash ever."

Christina looked at Margie. "I went to the Home Ec room at school. I showed the teacher the video of how to do the weaving, and we looked at pictures of some of the finished sashes and figured out what kind of thread I needed. We found enough left over from other projects, and I decided to make it right away and not wait to go to Michaels. I just finished it tonight. And you were here, so..."

"You're amazing," Margie told her tenderly. She was so proud of her daughter for knowing the right thing to do, and then just doing it.

"Tell me about it," Moushoom told Christina again.

Christina looked back at Moushoom and touched the sash. "The blue is from the flag, and from the rivers. The St. Lawrence River we came from, and the Bow River where you settled. The red is for the Red River Resistance and the blood that was spilled. And the white is for the infinity symbol, our connection to our mixed cultures and the Creator." She looked up into Moushoom's face, hopeful, waiting for his response.

"It is perfect," Moushoom told her. "You have learned much about your culture. Your skill with the thread... my sweetheart had very clever fingers. She was very good with thread and made many sashes and other projects. She would be very happy at your work."

Christina beamed. She smiled and gave him another hug.

"And this is like a hug from me that you can keep with you all the time," she said, giving the sash one last tug to straighten it. "Even when I'm not here."

"Yes. But the ones I get when you are here are always better."

RILEY PARK

*R*iley Park is one of Calgary's first parks to include a wading pool, built in 1913. The author recalls wading there in the updated pool built in about 1980.

P.D. Workman also remembers swinging on the swings for what seemed like hours and her father trying to get pictures of the gray squirrel that lived in Riley Park and ran along the telephone lines before the explosion of the squirrel population in Calgary. The eastern gray squirrels are an invasive species; a couple of them gifted to the zoo in the 1930s escaped and bred to cover the entire city, the estimated population now 100,000 or more. Most of the gray squirrels in Calgary are actually black in color.

The cricket pitch in Riley Park was apparently established and in use in 1908, before the park was officially established in 1910. Prairie Winds Park (see Grounded in the Wind) and Riley Park are two of the eight parks with cricket pitches in Calgary.

While the botanical study gardens mentioned in this story are fictional, there are some beautiful flower gardens in

Riley Park and an amazing variety of trees. The Senator Patrick Burns Memorial Rock Garden was built with over 20,000 pieces of flagstone salvaged from the senator's 18-room mansion.

Did you enjoy this book? Reviews and recommendations are vital to making a book successful.

Please leave a review at your favorite book store or review site and share it with your friends.

Don't miss the following bonus material:
Get your Parks Pat Survival Pack
Meet my other sleuths
Sign up for mailing list to get a free copy of Gluten-Free Murder
Other books by P.D. Workman
Learn more about the author

Get the Parks Pat Survival Pack!

Sign up for my newsletter and receive the **exclusive Parks Pat Survival Pack**, packed with bonus materials and extra goodies you won't find anywhere else.

Stay in the loop on new releases, special offers, and insider content—all delivered straight to your inbox.

Sign up today and start your adventure with Parks Pat!

https://shop.pdworkman.com/products/parks-pat-survival-pack

Here's what's inside:
• Out with the Sunset (Book 1, eBook)
Begin Margie's journey with her first gripping case as a Calgary homicide officer in the Parks Pat Mysteries.

- **Out with the Sunset (Book 1, Audiobook – Computer Narrated)**

Take the mystery on the go—perfect for your commute, workout, or a walk through the park.

- **Bonus Prequel Story: *Flight of the Bluejay***

Discover Margie's *true beginning*. Before she was a sleuth, she was a pregnant teen on the streets—fighting to survive and find her place in the world.

- **Discover Calgary's Treasures – Photo Minibook**

Step into the beauty of Calgary with this exclusive photo album showcasing the first 15 parks that inspired the series.

- **Digital Wallpapers**

Bring the beauty of Calgary's parks to your phone, tablet, or computer with stunning photography.

More *Parks Pat Mysteries* are on the way. In the meantime, check out one of these other sleuths at **pdworkman.com** or your favorite online retailer!

Erin Price, proprietor of Auntie Clem's Bakery and reluctant sleuth:
Gluten-Free Murder

Reg Rawlins, Psychic Investigator, is Erin's former foster sister:
What the Cat Knew

Zachary Goldman is a private investigator who fights demons of a different sort:
She Wore Mourning

Kenzie Kirsch, Zachary's romantic interest, cuts into crime in a medical thriller series: **Unlawful Harvest**

Gabriel and Renata fight against injustice their own way in this young adult series:
Mito

DON'T MISS A THING! GET THE LATEST NEWS AND A FREE EBOOK

Your First Taste

PDWORKMAN.COM/SIGNUP

ABOUT THE AUTHOR

P.D. Workman is a USA Today Bestselling author and multi-award winner, renowned for her prolific output of over 100 published works that span various genres. With a knack for crafting page-turners, Workman captivates readers with everything from cozy mysteries like the Auntie Clem's Bakery series to gripping young adult and suspense novels.

A prolific reader and writer since childhood, P.D. Workman crafts emotionally powerful stories that don't shy away from hard topics. Her books tackle mental illness, addiction, abuse, and trauma with raw honesty and compassion, giving voice to the often unheard. If you crave authentic, character-driven page-turners that hit deep and stay with you long after the final page, you're in the right place.

With each new release, fans eagerly anticipate another thrilling blend of thought-provoking storytelling and relatable characters that define P.D. Workman's brand as an author of unforgettable page-turners—gripping tales that leave a lasting impact long after the last page is turned.

> P. D. Workman, does not shy from probing the deep psychological scars of childhood trauma, mental illness, and addiction. Also characteristic of this author, these extremely sensitive issues are explored with extensive empathy, described with incredible clarity, and portrayed with profound insight.

Some of Workman's titles have been translated into Spanish, French, Portuguese, German, and Italian.

Workman began writing at an early age and is a prolific reader as well as writer. She is also passionate about teaching and learning, expresses her creativity through art and cooking, and loves exploring the Calgary parks and green spaces where the Parks Pat Mysteries are set. She was a legal assistant for many years and has done extensive charitable work.

Workman was born and raised in Alberta, Canada, and is married with one adult son.

Please visit P.D. Workman at pdworkman.com to see what else she is working on, to join her mailing list, and to link to her social networks.

If you enjoyed this book, please take the time to recommend it to other purchasers with a review or star rating and share it with your friends!

Find P.D. Workman's books at

PDWORKMAN.COM

Scan the QR code below

www.ingramcontent.com/pod-product-compliance
Lightning Source LLC
Chambersburg PA
CBHW031607260626
47154CB00020B/1703